Beyond the]
By Mohamed F
"Breaking Boundaries"

Copyright Page

© [2024], [Mohamed Elshenawy]

All rights reserved.

No part of this publication may be reproduced, distributed, or transmitted in any form or by any means, including photocopying, recording, or other electronic or mechanical methods, without the prior written permission of the publisher, except in the case of brief quotations embodied in critical reviews and certain other noncommercial uses permitted by copyright law.

First Published: [2024]

Publisher: [Mohamed Elshenawy "Self-Published"]

This is a work of fiction. Names, characters, places, and incidents are either products of the author's imagination or used fictitiously. Any resemblance to actual events, locales, or persons, living or dead, is entirely coincidental.

Table of Contents

Introduction to "Beyond the Ice Wall""Breaking Boundaries"......... 1
About the Author: [Mohamed Elshenawy]...2
"Breaking Boundaries" 3
The big lie 24
The Awakening..38
Interrogation..43
A Moment of Chaos 49
The Great Escape 55
The Resistance 67
The Science of War..73
Breaking the Enemy 79
The Turning Point 85
The Return and the Chase 91
Author's Note:..96
More to Come: 97

Introduction to "Beyond the Ice Wall""Breaking Boundaries"

For generations, we have looked to the stars, believing the answers to our greatest mysteries lay in the vast expanse of the universe. But what if the truth has been much closer all along, hidden behind boundaries we were never meant to cross?

Dr. Ethan Cole, a brilliant scientist working for NASA, was drawn into a top-secret project—unlocking the power of a Stargate believed to transport humans to distant planets. What he didn't expect was for the gate to lead him to a hidden realm right here on Earth. Beyond the frozen ice wall, Cole discovers a reality that shatters everything he knows about our world.

Joined by investigative journalist Lena and a rebellious group of green-skinned inhabitants, Cole finds himself in a battle for survival against the Reptilians, powerful beings who control this hidden realm. As he uncovers the shocking truth about the Controllers—ancient forces manipulating humanity for centuries—Cole must decide how far he's willing to go to expose a truth that may be too dangerous to reveal.

Beyond the Ice Wall is an epic journey of discovery, mystery, and survival. It explores the boundaries between reality and conspiracy, blending science fiction with mind-bending revelations. The more you uncover, the more you question what's real—and what's not.

Prepare for an adventure where science, myth, and cosmic forces collide. This is not just a battle for survival; it's a battle for the truth.

About the Author: [Mohamed Elshenawy]

I am Mohamed Elshenawy, a passionate writer of science fiction, horror and fantasy, with a love for weaving intricate stories that blend the speculative with the mysterious. My works often challenge the boundaries of reality, exploring themes of conspiracy, hidden truths, and the vast unknowns of our universe.

Alongside writing, I bring a diverse background as a. Fluent in multiple languages, I draw inspiration from global cultures, myths, and science, creating stories that resonate with readers from all walks of life.

In *Beyond the Ice Wall*, I aim to take readers on an unforgettable journey that questions everything we think we know about our world—and the forces that control it.

"Breaking Boundaries"

Late Night at NASA

The hum of fluorescent lights echoed softly in the empty hallways of NASA's research facility. It was a sound I had grown all too accustomed to over the years. I glanced at the clock on the far wall of my lab—3:27 AM. Another late night. No, who am I kidding? Another late morning.

The room was cluttered with schematics, half-empty coffee cups, and diagrams of dimensional physics, each more complex than the last. The soft hum of computers and the occasional flicker of the monitors were the only companions I had at this hour. I'd chosen this isolation. Ten years—ten long years of failure after failure had led me here, to this moment of near-breakthrough.

The Stargate Project. A concept that had lived only in the minds of visionaries and lunatics, now standing before me as an almost-complete reality. The idea had once been simple: a gateway, a portal to the stars, capable of instantaneously transporting matter from one point in the universe to another. Travel to distant planets, explore the far reaches of the cosmos, all without ever leaving the ground. The implications were revolutionary.

Except it didn't work. Or rather, it hadn't. Not yet.

I ran a hand through my thinning hair, eyes fixated on the digital screen in front of me. Data streamed endlessly, calculations that had begun to blur together over the years. I could feel it in my gut—the solution was close, but the final piece kept eluding me. Every night I promised myself the same thing: this would be the breakthrough, the night I cracked it. And every night I left empty-handed, clutching at the same hope like a lifeline.

I stood up and walked over to the large, circular ring at the center of the lab. The Stargate.

The device stood nearly eight feet tall, a metallic frame inlaid with circuits and glowing runes that seemed to pulse with life. It was beautiful in its way, a triumph of engineering, and yet its secrets remained buried beneath layers of complex physics I couldn't yet decipher.

I took a deep breath, steeling myself for another round of tests. The gate had to work—there was no other option. After a decade of my life devoted to this project, failure was no longer an acceptable outcome.

"Okay... let's try this again."

My voice broke the silence, a futile attempt to convince myself that this time, this time would be different.

I typed a series of commands into the terminal, fingers moving with practiced precision. A low hum began to emanate from the gate, its once-dormant circuits lighting up, casting an eerie glow across the lab. The air in the room seemed to shift, thickening with a palpable tension as if the very atmosphere anticipated what was to come.

The ring began to spin, slowly at first, and then faster, the lights intensifying as the machine worked to align with some distant, uncharted point in space. I held my breath, waiting for the familiar flicker of failure that always came next.

But this time... nothing.

No failure. No shutdown. The gate continued to spin, its power rising, until the familiar ripple of energy shimmered into view within the ring's center.

My heart stopped. The gate had stabilized—no shutdown, no power failure.

It was working.

I took a step back, eyes wide, not fully processing what I was seeing. A shimmering pool of light now filled the ring, like liquid glass, rippling gently as if disturbed by an unseen hand. I stared into the glowing surface, feeling the pull of the unknown, of the endless possibilities that lay beyond.

But before I could react, the sound of my lab door opening jolted me out of my trance.

Lena Hayes Enters the Picture

I turned sharply, heart pounding, only to find the last person I expected to see.

"Dr. Cole, isn't it?"

The voice was calm, self-assured, and distinctly feminine. A woman stood in the doorway, her silhouette outlined by the harsh fluorescent light from the hallway. She stepped into the lab, closing the door quietly behind her. The intrusion was casual, as though she belonged here.

But she didn't.

Her eyes scanned the room, taking in every detail before landing on me. She was in her late twenties, early thirties maybe, with sharp features that suggested both intelligence and determination. Long dark hair framed her face, and there was something unsettling about the confidence in her gaze, like she knew more than she should.

"Who the hell are you?" I snapped, my nerves frayed from both the gate's success and the unexpected intrusion.

She smiled, and it wasn't a friendly one. "Lena Hayes. Journalist."

I stared at her, dumbfounded. A journalist. In my lab. At 3:30 in the goddamn morning.

"How did you get in here?" I demanded, anger replacing the initial shock. This lab was supposed to be secure, protected by layers of clearance and classified files. No one—especially no journalist—should have been able to waltz in here like she owned the place.

She ignored my question, her gaze shifting to the Stargate behind me. "What is that?" she asked, her voice dripping with curiosity. She stepped closer, peering at the rippling surface of the gate, as if drawn to it.

"Stop!" I moved quickly, blocking her path. The last thing I needed was an untrained civilian getting too close to something we barely understood. "You don't know what you're dealing with."

"Oh, but I do." She looked at me, her eyes glinting with a kind of predatory amusement. "You see, Dr. Cole, I've been following your work for quite some time."

I felt a cold chill run down my spine. "What are you talking about?"

She reached into her bag, pulling out a small recorder. "The Stargate Project," she said casually, as if she were discussing the weather. "You've been working on this for what—ten years now? A top-secret NASA project to open portals to other planets? Pretty ambitious, even for you."

I felt my heart rate spike. How the hell did she know about the project? Everything was classified, buried under layers of secrecy. Only a handful of people even knew it existed.

"I don't know what you think you know," I said, my voice low, "but you need to leave. Now."

She didn't budge. Instead, she arched an eyebrow, clearly unimpressed by my attempt to assert control over the situation.

"I think I know more than you'd like me to," she said coolly. "And I think I'm not the only one who's curious about what NASA's really been up to all these years."

My mind raced, trying to figure out how much she knew, how much of a threat she posed. Whoever Lena Hayes was, she was no ordinary journalist. She'd gotten too close—far too close to secrets that could destroy not only the project but everything I'd worked for.

"This isn't something you can just write about in a blog post," I warned her. "What we're dealing with here... it's beyond you."

Her expression softened, but only slightly. "Then why don't you enlighten me?"

Face-Off Between Lena and Dr. Cole

I could feel my pulse pounding in my ears, a slow boil of frustration building in my chest. The Stargate was stable, rippling and glowing behind me, but I couldn't focus on the success, not with her standing here.

Lena Hayes. A journalist? This was worse than I thought. People like her didn't just stumble into government facilities, let alone top-secret labs, without a reason.

Her eyes lingered on the Stargate, curiosity and something else—determination—shining in them. She looked back at me, as if she could read my thoughts.

"What is it, Dr. Cole? What are you so afraid of?" she asked, her voice calm and measured. It wasn't a question—more of a challenge.

"You don't belong here," I snapped, trying to regain some semblance of control. "Whatever you think you know, you're wrong. This is classified, and you're in way over your head."

"I don't think I am," she said, smiling faintly. "You see, I've been digging into this for months. At first, it was just rumors—NASA's secret experiments, unexplained anomalies, energy readings that made no sense. Then I found out about you." She nodded toward me as if I were a puzzle piece she'd finally placed.

"I don't know what you're talking about." The lie came easily, but it felt hollow. She already knew too much.

Lena crossed her arms, leaning against the edge of a nearby desk, all too comfortable in a place where she shouldn't be. "The Stargate Project," she repeated, and my gut twisted. "You've been trying to open a portal to other worlds, other dimensions. You think you've found a way to travel instantaneously across the universe."

Her words hit like a punch, not because they were wrong, but because they were too close to the truth. "You don't have any idea what this project is about," I muttered, my eyes narrowing.

"Then explain it to me," she shot back, her eyes blazing now. "Tell me I'm wrong."

I gritted my teeth, turning away from her. My mind was racing, trying to figure out how to get her out of here without making a scene. I glanced at the terminal, the screen still displaying the stable readings from the gate. The energy levels were holding, but for how long? This was the closest I'd ever gotten to success, and now this journalist was here, threatening to derail everything.

"I can't let you publish anything about this," I said, my voice a low growl. "You'll put yourself in danger—and not just from me."

She blinked at that, her expression shifting slightly. I could see her trying to read between the lines of what I had just said. "Danger?" she asked, voice laced with curiosity. "From who? NASA? The government?"

"There are things you don't understand," I warned her. "If you push too hard, you're going to get hurt."

Her lips twisted into a wry smile. "You're going to have to try harder than that to scare me, Dr. Cole."

I clenched my fists, feeling the frustration boil over. "What do you want?" I barked.

Lena's smile widened just slightly, knowing she'd gotten under my skin. "I want the truth, Dr. Cole. That's all. I think the public has a right to know what NASA's been hiding."

"You don't know what you're asking for," I said, shaking my head.

"Then show me."

The room went silent for a moment, the only sound the soft hum of the Stargate behind me. Her words hung in the air, a challenge I couldn't ignore.

Show her?

I stared at her, weighing my options. I could try to force her out, but she'd already seen too much. If she was as relentless as she seemed, she wouldn't stop until she had what she wanted. And yet... if I showed her the truth, would that silence her, or would it drag her in deeper?

"You don't understand what you're asking for," I repeated, more to myself than to her.

"Then help me understand."

Lena's Relentlessness

The silence stretched between us, heavy and charged. Lena didn't move. She just stood there, calm, her eyes locked on mine, refusing to back down. She knew she had me. She could feel the tension in the air, and she was using it to her advantage.

I rubbed a hand over my face, trying to think clearly, but the last several hours of work had left me drained. The gateway was still open, waiting. It beckoned with the soft shimmer of liquid light, the portal to another world—maybe another planet, maybe something far worse. This was the breakthrough I had worked my entire career for, but I couldn't focus on it, not with her here.

I turned to face her fully. "You have no idea what you're getting into."

She raised an eyebrow, unimpressed. "I've been tracking this for months. I think I know more than you think."

"Do you? Do you really?" My voice was sharper now, the frustration bleeding into every word. "Do you know what's out there? What we've uncovered?"

Her expression faltered for just a moment, but then the steely resolve returned. "I know that you've been lying to the world, hiding something that could change everything. And I know that you're afraid—afraid of the truth, afraid of what happens next. But the public deserves to know, and I'm going to make sure they do."

I sighed, turning my back on her, staring at the swirling portal before me. It was mesmerizing, the way the light danced across its surface, the ripples of energy distorting the air around it. I had been chasing this moment for years, and now I was standing on the precipice of discovery. But that discovery came with a price.

"I'm not afraid of the truth," I said quietly. "I'm afraid of what happens when it's set loose."

Lena didn't respond. Instead, I heard the soft click of her recorder as she turned it off and slipped it back into her bag. "Show me," she said again, her voice more certain now. "Show me what you've been working on."

I hesitated. This wasn't just some story—this was the kind of knowledge that could break someone. Lena didn't know it yet, but she was on the edge of something far greater than she realized.

Hours had passed since the encounter with Lena, and I hadn't seen her leave the facility. I had assumed she was long gone, but as the night stretched into early morning, I couldn't shake the feeling that something was wrong. I stayed late—later than usual—pouring over my data, tweaking the algorithms, recalibrating the machines. The Stargate was still stable, but I needed to understand why. Was it a fluke? A random event?

Then, as if the universe was conspiring against me, I heard a sound. A faint rustling. My skin prickled. The facility was empty—or at least it was supposed to be.

I turned slowly, scanning the room. For a moment, I saw nothing. But then I spotted movement in the shadows near the far end of the lab, near my desk. Lena. She was here. Again.

I cursed under my breath. How had she gotten in? And more importantly, what did she think she was going to find?

Quietly, I moved toward her, intending to confront her once and for all. But before I could say anything, she turned, and we locked eyes.

She didn't look scared. No, if anything, she looked more determined than ever.

"You're making a mistake," I warned, my voice low.

She shook her head. "No. You are. You think you can keep this secret forever, but you can't."

The tension between us was suffocating, and before I could stop her, Lena moved toward the Stargate. "What is this?" she asked, her eyes wide with fascination. "You really did it, didn't you?"

"Lena, don't—"

But it was too late. She reached out, her fingers brushing the surface of the portal, and in that instant, the Stargate responded. The liquid surface rippled violently, glowing brighter, almost as if it was reacting to her presence.

Before I could react, the entire room shifted. The walls seemed to bend inward, the lights flickering wildly, and the air became thick, charged with energy. My heart raced. The gate was reacting—something was happening, something I couldn't control.

"Get away from it!" I shouted, rushing toward her.

But she didn't listen. She stood there, transfixed, her eyes locked on the glowing surface. And then, before I could stop her, she stepped forward—right into the Stargate.

The moment Lena's fingers brushed the surface of the Stargate, the room seemed to shift—like reality itself was bending around us. The lights flickered, and the gentle hum of the machines grew louder, vibrating with a strange intensity that hadn't been there before. The air felt charged, as if something had awakened.

"Lena!" I shouted, trying to reach her before things spiraled completely out of control.

But she was standing there, mesmerized by the rippling liquid surface of the gate. For a moment, I thought she might step through, and the fear of losing her—or worse, letting her drag something back with her—sent a jolt of panic through me.

I grabbed her arm, yanking her back from the gate. "What are you doing? You have no idea what's on the other side!"

She looked at me, eyes wide, half in awe and half in defiance. "And neither do you."

I exhaled sharply, realizing she was right. As much as I hated to admit it, I was no more certain of what lay beyond the gate than she was. All I had were theories. The gate was a one-way passage, but to where? And for how long? The unknown beckoned, both thrilling and terrifying.

"I'm going through," she said, her voice steady despite the tremor in the air. "And I'm taking you with me."

I stared at her, incredulous. "You have no idea what could be on the other side. The atmosphere, the environment—it could be deadly. We need to prepare."

Lena raised an eyebrow. "Then let's prepare."

Suited Up for the Unknown

The logical part of my brain kicked in. If we were going through the gate, we couldn't just dive in recklessly. The idea that the other side might not support human life was a very real possibility, and as much as I was curious, I wasn't suicidal.

I pointed to the far side of the lab, where several lockers were lined up against the wall. "We'll need suits. NASA equipment. And oxygen tanks. I'm not risking stepping into a toxic atmosphere or a vacuum."

Lena gave me a small nod, then followed as I led the way to the lockers. Inside were NASA's standard issue environmental suits—designed for extraterrestrial exploration. The suits were equipped with built-in life support systems, including oxygen tanks and temperature control, meant to withstand harsh, unpredictable conditions. I had used them in simulations, but this was no simulation. This was real.

I handed her one of the suits, and she eyed it for a moment, then started putting it on without hesitation. I did the same, fastening the seals, double-checking the oxygen supply and making sure everything was functioning properly.

Focus. Stay calm.

I repeated the mantra to myself as I secured the helmet over my head. The soft hiss of air filled my ears, the pressure of the suit settling in like a second skin. Lena followed suit, suiting up without complaint, though her hands trembled slightly as she adjusted the oxygen tank.

"Have you ever done anything like this before?" I asked, the tension between us shifting slightly as the situation grew more serious.

"No," she admitted, her voice coming through the suit's built-in comm system. "But there's a first time for everything."

"Not usually something you want to say when stepping into an interdimensional portal," I muttered under my breath.

Lena chuckled, though the sound was hollow inside the helmet. "I've taken worse risks."

I doubted that. Nothing could compare to what we were about to do.

Once we were fully suited, I turned back to the gate, which still shimmered and rippled with a surreal, otherworldly light. My heart was pounding in my chest, the enormity of what we were about to do hitting me all at once.

"This is insane," yes the gate always returns you to Earth I said, more to myself than to her. "but I'm not sure if there's a way back."

"You said the gate always returns you to Earth, right?" Lena asked.

"In theory," I replied, my voice tight. "But I've never gone through it. No one has."

"Well, now's your chance."

She stepped forward, her gloved hand reaching out once more toward the shimmering surface of the portal. I wanted to stop her, wanted to tell her to wait, but the truth was, I couldn't resist the pull either. Every part of my mind screamed at me to stay put, to retreat, but the obsession—the need to know—was stronger.

Without another word, I followed her, and together, we stepped through the Stargate.

Through the Stargate

It was like being submerged in ice water, but without the cold. The sensation was jarring, disorienting, as if we were being pulled through a thin membrane between two realities. I couldn't see, couldn't feel anything but the pull, and then—suddenly—it was over.

The world came back into focus.

The first thing I noticed was the sky—a sickly, dim greenish-gray, with no clear source of light. The sun, if there was one, was hidden behind a thick veil of clouds. The air was still, unnervingly so, as though the atmosphere itself was waiting for something to happen.

I blinked, my helmet fogging slightly as I tried to adjust to the strange surroundings. We were standing on what looked like soft earth, but the ground felt wrong beneath my boots, too soft, almost spongy. The landscape stretched out before us—endless fields of tall, dark grass swaying gently despite the lack of wind. In the distance, I could make out twisted trees, their branches gnarled and leafless, like skeletal fingers clawing at the sky.

"Where the hell are we?" Lena asked, her voice echoing through the comm system.

"I... I don't know." My own voice was hoarse, the reality of the situation sinking in. "I've never seen anything like this."

The portal behind us shimmered faintly, but it was clear—this was no ordinary place. It felt... ancient. Old beyond comprehension. There was a weight to the air, something oppressive that pressed down on my chest, making it hard to breathe, even with the suit.

Lena stepped forward, scanning the horizon. "Is this another planet?"

"I don't think so," I said, shaking my head. "The data... it doesn't match anything we've ever recorded. It feels... off."

Lena glanced back at me. "Off how?"

"Like we're not supposed to be here."

I turned slowly, taking in the surroundings, and that's when I saw it—a village in the distance, partially obscured by the mist that seemed to hang over everything. The buildings were old, crumbling, made of stone and wood, like something out of the 12th century.

"That village," Lena said, noticing it at the same time. "It looks abandoned."

"That's not a good sign—it proves there are creatures lurking in this place. Something about it felt deeply unsettling, and I couldn't shake the eerie sensation that we were being watched."

We started toward the village, moving cautiously. The ground seemed to shift beneath our feet with every step, but there was no other choice. We had no idea where we were, or how long the Stargate would remain open.

As we approached the village, the feeling of being watched intensified. I glanced around, scanning the shadows between the trees and the dilapidated buildings, but saw nothing. Still, the hair on the back of my neck stood on end.

And then we saw them.

Two figures, standing at the edge of the village, partially hidden by the mist. They were small—children, by the looks of them—and their skin... their skin was a strange, sickly green.

Lena stopped dead in her tracks, and I felt my heart skip a beat.

"What the hell?" she whispered.

The children didn't move. They just stood there, watching us with eyes that seemed too large for their faces, their expressions unreadable. I took a step closer, my breath fogging the inside of my helmet as I tried to get a better look.

"Dr. Cole," Lena said quietly. "Do you see what I see?"

"Yeah," I muttered, my voice tight. "I see it."

The children didn't speak. They just stared at us, unmoving, unblinking. And then, slowly, one of them raised a hand, pointing toward the center of the village.

"We need to go," Lena whispered, her voice tense.

But something told me we were already too late.

The children didn't move. They stood there, statuesque, their eyes reflecting the faint, sickly light from the sky. Something about them felt wrong, unnatural—their greenish skin, their small, frail forms, and the stillness that surrounded them like a shadow.

"Who are they?" Lena asked, her voice hushed, like she didn't want the question to carry.

I shook my head. "I don't know. But this doesn't feel right."

The air around us was thick, heavy, as if something unseen was pressing down on us, making every breath a little harder to take. My suit's oxygen supply hissed quietly in my ears, but the tightness in my chest wasn't coming from lack of air. It was the feeling of being watched, of being judged by something far beyond our understanding.

Lena stepped forward cautiously, her hand resting on her helmet, as if considering removing it. "Maybe they're lost," she suggested, but there was no conviction in her voice.

I grabbed her arm, pulling her back. "Don't. We don't know what's in the air here. Keep your suit sealed."

She hesitated, then nodded. "Right. Sorry."

We stood there, watching the children, unsure of what to do next. That's when it happened.

Without warning, the children screamed.

It wasn't the cry of a child lost or in pain. No, this was something primal, raw—a piercing, high-pitched wail that cut through the air like a blade, making every nerve in my body flare with fear. The sound was unnatural, distorted, like it came from deep within their throats but carried the weight of something much older, much darker.

Lena recoiled, her hands instinctively going to cover her ears inside her helmet, even though the suit muffled the sound. "What the hell is happening?" she gasped, her voice shaking.

I wanted to answer her, but the scream was so overwhelming, so invasive, it was all I could do to remain standing. My eyes locked on the children, their faces contorted, mouths wide open, releasing this otherworldly cry that seemed to vibrate through the very ground beneath us.

And then, just as suddenly as it had begun, the scream stopped.

The silence that followed was deafening. My heart pounded in my chest, my breath coming in short, ragged gasps. I could feel sweat beading on my forehead beneath my helmet, and for a moment, I thought I might pass out from the sheer tension.

But that's when I saw them.

Emerging from the mist that clung to the edges of the village, figures began to appear—silent, motionless, watching us with eyes that seemed to glow faintly in the dim light. They were like the children, but larger. Adults. Their skin the same sickly green hue, their bodies tall and thin, clothed in rags and strange woven fabrics that looked ancient, yet functional.

They surrounded us.

Surrounded by the Green People

Lena took a step back, her breath quickening as more of the green-skinned people emerged from the shadows. There were dozens of them, all with the same blank, unreadable expressions, their eyes wide and unblinking. They formed a loose circle around us, cutting off any path of escape.

"We need to get out of here," Lena whispered, but her voice was tinged with fear, as though she knew there was nowhere to run.

I raised a hand, trying to show them we weren't a threat. "We don't mean you any harm," I said, my voice steady but my heart racing. I wasn't sure if they could understand me, but it was all I could do to remain calm.

The green-skinned villagers didn't react. They just stood there, their eyes fixed on us, their stillness unnerving. The children had fallen silent, standing at the front of the group like sentinels, their heads tilted slightly, as if they were waiting for something.

Suddenly, one of the taller figures stepped forward. He was older than the others, his face lined with wrinkles, but his eyes held the same eerie glow. He wore a cloak of rough, tattered fabric, and there was a kind of authority in his bearing that marked him as someone important.

The chieftain, I realized. Their leader.

He looked at us for a long moment, his eyes narrowing slightly as they moved from me to Lena, then back again. His gaze lingered on our suits, the NASA emblem emblazoned on our chests, and something seemed to shift in his expression. Recognition.

Before I could say anything, he spoke.

The chieftain's voice was deep, gravelly, and the language he spoke was like nothing I had ever heard. It was harsh, guttural, with strange consonants and sounds that seemed to echo off the walls of the crumbling buildings around us. Whatever it was, it wasn't any language I had come across in my years of study. Lena, beside me, shook her head, clearly as lost as I was.

"What is he saying?" she asked, her voice tense.

"I don't know," I replied, frustration gnawing at me. "It doesn't match any language I've encountered. But... I think he knows something."

The chieftain's eyes narrowed further, and he spoke again, this time louder, more insistent. The green-skinned villagers behind him shifted slightly, their eyes flicking toward the pit at the center of the village, then back to us. There was a sense of urgency in their movements, like they were waiting for something to happen.

I glanced at Lena, my mind racing. We had to figure out what they wanted—why they had surrounded us, why they hadn't attacked or fled.

But then, the chieftain's eyes locked onto our suits again, and his next words sent a cold chill down my spine.

"Area 51."

The words were unmistakable, clear as day despite the thick accent that coated them. Lena's eyes went wide, and I could feel the blood drain from my face.

"How does he know about Area 51?" Lena whispered, her voice trembling with disbelief.

I had no answer.

Taken to the Village

The chieftain barked an order, and two of the larger villagers stepped forward, motioning for us to follow. They didn't appear hostile, but there was no mistaking the command in their eyes. We were to go with them.

"I don't think we have a choice," I muttered to Lena.

She nodded, her face pale behind the visor of her helmet. "Area 51? What the hell does that mean?"

"I don't know," I said, feeling the weight of the situation pressing down on me. "But we need to find out."

We followed the villagers through the misty village, past crumbling stone buildings and twisted trees, their gnarled branches stretching out like claws toward the dim sky. The air was thick with the smell of damp earth and something metallic, almost like blood. My heart raced, every instinct screaming at me to turn back, but there was no going back now. We were too far in.

The villagers led us to the largest building in the village—a structure made of stone and wood, ancient and crumbling but still standing. Inside, the air was cooler, and the walls were lined with strange symbols carved deep into the stone, symbols that pulsed faintly with a soft, greenish light.

The chieftain stepped forward, his eyes scanning us once more. He spoke again, his voice low and filled with a strange intensity.

"Area 51," he repeated, pointing at our suits. "You... from there."

I stared at him, trying to piece together what he was saying, but my mind was racing too fast. How could they know about Area 51?

How could this ancient, seemingly primitive village in another world possibly have any connection to one of the most secretive military bases on Earth?

Suddenly, a figure emerged from the shadows—a woman, human, but her presence here made no sense. My heart skipped a beat. She looked familiar. Too familiar. Dark hair, sharp features, and eyes that held a glint of recognition. But I couldn't place where I'd seen her before.

"Take off your helmets," she said calmly, in perfect English.

Lena and I exchanged a glance. "What?" Lena asked, her voice muffled through her helmet.

"There's oxygen here," the woman explained, stepping closer. "Just like any other place on Earth. You don't need those."

I hesitated, instinctively protective of my suit, but something about her confidence—her familiarity—made me comply. Slowly, I unclasped the locks on my helmet and lifted it off, feeling the cool, damp air of the village settle around me. Lena did the same, her expression mirroring the confusion I felt.

The air was breathable, as promised. But that wasn't the only shock.

The woman smiled softly. "My name is Sarah," she said, her voice steady. "I'll translate. There's a lot you need to know."

Lena narrowed her eyes, stepping forward. "Who are you? How do you speak English?"

Sarah's smile faded slightly. "I'm... like you," she said cryptically, then turned to the chieftain, who had been watching us in silence.

The chieftain spoke again in that strange, guttural language, his voice low and steady. The villagers around us remained still, their eyes reflecting the dim light of the chamber, watching us with an intensity that made my skin crawl.

Sarah began to translate.

The Truth Revealed

"We are the **green race**, but we are not different from you," Sarah said, her tone calm but serious. "We are as human as any other race. Long ago, we lived alongside the other human races, in what you call **Area 51**."

I frowned, the familiar name sparking a flood of questions in my mind, but Sarah continued before I could speak.

"Area 51 is what you know as planet Earth. Every continent, every part of the sphere you're familiar with—it's all Area 51. We were placed there long before the boundaries were drawn,". "Before the ice walls rose, dividing the realm into separate sections. We were one of many races, but... we were relocated. Moved to Area 52. Cut off from technology, from knowledge, from everything that defined us. Forced to start over—as slaves."

Lena's mouth fell open, and she shook her head in disbelief. "Slaves? Who... who did this to you?"

The chieftain spoke again, his voice a harsh rasp. Sarah's expression darkened as she translated.

"The ones who control our realm," she said. "They exist in all areas, all over the world. **The Controllers.** They are not human, but they walk among us, and they manipulate every part of our reality. We... were placed here to serve them."

The room felt colder suddenly, the oppressive weight of her words sinking in. My mind reeled as I tried to piece together the implications of what she was saying. The "realm?" Ice walls? Controllers? None of it made sense, and yet... there was something in Sarah's eyes that told me this was more than just a strange myth.

Lena stepped forward, her voice shaky. "Wait—who are these 'Controllers'? What do they control? And why Area 51?"

Sarah turned to her, her gaze steady. "Each area is controlled by different forces," she said, her voice soft. "In our area, it is the **Reptilians**."

I froze, the word hitting me like a sledgehammer. **Reptilians**. I had heard whispers of them before—wild conspiracy theories, stories passed around by fringe groups, dismissed by every credible scientist I'd ever worked with. Shape-shifting reptilian overlords who controlled humanity from behind the scenes. I had always thought it was nonsense. Until now.

The chieftain spoke again, his voice growing more animated, and Sarah's face darkened as she translated his words.

"They control us. They... shape-shift, change their appearance, blending in with any race, any form," she said. "We fought back. We tried to resist, but their power... their technology... it's too strong. They are impossible to defeat."

Lena shook her head in disbelief. "Reptilians? Are you serious? You're telling me this is... real?"

Sarah's eyes softened with a kind of sad understanding. "I know how it sounds. But I've lived it. We've lived it."

The chieftain continued, his voice rising with a kind of quiet desperation. Sarah translated, her tone heavy with emotion.

"They have placed us in these villages, keeping us here... only so we can continue to serve them. They control the technology, the resources, everything. We are trapped here, slowly dying out. Our race... is headed for extinction."

Lena and I stood there, speechless, the weight of the revelation pressing down on us like a physical force. Extinction. A race of people trapped in a forgotten realm, enslaved by shape-shifting overlords? It sounded like a nightmare—a fever dream. But the fear in Sarah's eyes told me it was all too real.

I swallowed hard, my voice barely a whisper. "What do you want from us?"

Sarah looked directly at me, her gaze intense. "We need help. The science and technology from **Area 51**—what you have access to. It's the only chance we have left. You... you have the knowledge, the tools. Maybe... only maybe... you can help us fight back."

My mind raced, trying to process everything. The gate, the reptilians, the enslaved green-skinned people... it was all too much. I felt the ground shift beneath me, my vision swimming with the sheer impossibility of it all.

Lena, however, seemed to find her voice. "Wait—how can we help? You're asking us to fight shape-shifters? With... what? We barely even know where we are!"

Sarah nodded solemnly. "I know. But you're the first outsiders we've seen in generations. You are from Area 51. They control the science. The technology. You must have some way of accessing it. Or at least... you have minds that can help us find a way."

My mouth went dry. The weight of what she was asking—what they were all asking—settled in my chest like a boulder. How could we help them? We were just two people, lost in a world we didn't understand, up against forces that defied everything I thought I knew about the universe.

But there was no denying the desperation in the villagers' eyes. They had been fighting for survival, for their freedom, for who knew how long. And they were looking to us as their last hope.

Lena looked at me, her expression a mixture of disbelief and determination. "Dr. Cole... what do we do?"

I stared back at her, my mind reeling with the impossible decision laid before us.

"I don't know," I said finally, my voice hoarse. "But we're in this now. And I don't think we have a choice."

The big lie

The air in the stone chamber felt thick, almost suffocating. My helmet was off, the coolness of the room mingling with the sweat on my forehead. It wasn't the temperature that unsettled me, though—it was the words. The impossible words Sarah had just spoken. They buzzed in my ears like a swarm of angry bees, their meaning refusing to settle in my mind.

"We are from Area 51," Sarah had said. "But... everything you know about that place, about the universe... it's all wrong."

I shook my head, refusing to let the full weight of her statement sink in. "No," I muttered, more to myself than to her. "That's... that's ridiculous. This—this can't be right."

Lena, standing beside me, crossed her arms, her expression one of disbelief and frustration. "Wait a minute," she said, her voice sharp. "You're saying there are no other planets? No space? You're telling me NASA—every scientist on Earth—has been lying? That doesn't make any sense."

Sarah remained calm, her eyes steady as she looked at us. "They aren't lying," she said softly. "They just don't know."

"What?" I felt my pulse quicken, my mind spinning. "What are you even saying? I've dedicated my life to science—to understanding the universe. We've sent probes, satellites, people into space! I've seen the data, the images. The universe is... it's vast. There are billions of stars, planets, galaxies..."

Sarah smiled gently, but it was a smile laced with sadness. "That's what they want you to believe. That's what you've been taught. But it's not real."

I stepped back, shaking my head more vigorously, trying to cling to something, anything, that made sense. "No. No, that's impossible. The physics alone—the calculations—the curvature of the Earth! Space exists! I've spent my entire life studying it."

Lena, though clearly disturbed, wasn't willing to accept this either. "What about astronauts? People have been to the moon. We've seen it. People can look through telescopes and see other planets. Are you seriously saying all of that is fake?"

Sarah's expression didn't waver. "Not fake. Misunderstood. What you see, what you've been shown—it's part of the system of control. The Earth is… much larger than you've been told. There are no planets, no galaxies beyond. Just the Earth—endless, vast, without boundaries, but divided."

"Divided?" I snapped, my voice louder than I intended. "Divided by what?"

Sarah glanced at the chieftain, who stood silently, his green eyes glowing faintly in the dim light. She then turned back to us, her voice softer now, as if explaining a deep, ancient truth. "By the **Controllers**. They built the **ice walls**, separating the Earth into different areas, each one isolated from the others. You've been led to believe that Earth is just one small planet in a massive universe. But the truth is… the Earth is the universe. There is no space beyond it."

The room felt like it was spinning. My head swam as Sarah's words collided with everything I had spent my life believing. "No, that's not… that doesn't fit with any of the laws of physics, with anything we know about the universe."

Sarah tilted her head slightly, her gaze unwavering. "Who do you think taught you those laws?"

I blinked, feeling the ground tilt beneath me. "What?"

"The **Controllers**," she said. "They control everything—your science, your education, your governments. They have fed humanity a false reality, keeping you all trapped within the boundaries of the Earth without ever knowing the truth."

Lena let out a harsh laugh, a sound filled with disbelief. "Okay, hold on. Are you telling us that the entire human race is living in some kind of giant… bubble? And that the universe is just… Earth?"

"Yes," Sarah said quietly. "A realm with no boundaries, no limits—except those imposed by the Controllers. They've kept humanity divided, in the dark, for thousands of years."

"No," I said, my voice trembling with anger now. "That's insane. You're talking about... what? A conspiracy on a global scale? No. Larger than global—universal! This doesn't make sense! The moon landings, the space stations, the satellites—everything we've done to explore space. How do you explain that?"

Sarah stepped closer, her voice calm but insistent. "You've never been to space. None of you have. The Controllers manipulate what you see, what you experience. The sky—the stars—they are projections, illusions designed to keep you believing in a false reality."

I couldn't breathe. My chest tightened as if the air had been sucked out of the room. Projections? Illusions? It sounded... insane. This was the kind of thing conspiracy theorists babbled about on fringe websites. And yet, standing here in this strange, otherworldly village, with people who clearly didn't fit into any known history or civilization... I couldn't deny the possibility that there was more at play than I understood.

But I refused to let go. "No," I said again, though the conviction in my voice was faltering. "I've seen the stars. I've studied them. The distance between Earth and other planets, the speed of light, the cosmic background radiation—there's too much evidence. You can't just explain all of that away."

Sarah nodded. "I understand why it's difficult to accept. Your entire life has been built on these ideas. But the Controllers have more power than you can imagine. They've shaped your reality—your understanding of the world, of the universe—so that you remain trapped in your area, believing that there's nothing else."

"The **firmament**," Sarah continued, her eyes growing more intense as she spoke. "It surrounds this realm. It's an impenetrable barrier that even the Controllers cannot cross. It's what keeps us all here, separated in these different areas. No one—not even the most powerful Controllers—can pass through it."

Lena's face twisted in disbelief. "So, what? You're saying that all of our technology, all the science that's been developed over centuries, is just wrong? That the Earth isn't a planet at all, but some kind of... contained world, broken up into sections?"

"Exactly," Sarah said.

I took a step back, my breath coming in ragged gasps. The room felt like it was closing in around me. "No... this can't be..."

Sarah looked at me with a kind of quiet empathy. "I know it's hard to accept, Dr. Cole. You've built your life on the pursuit of knowledge, of understanding the universe. But the truth is, the universe isn't what you think it is. Earth... is all there is. And it's been divided and controlled for centuries."

I wanted to scream, to shout that it wasn't true. But the words wouldn't come. Instead, I found myself spiraling deeper into a sense of confusion, of loss. Everything I had studied, everything I had worked for, everything I believed—was it all a lie? Was my entire understanding of reality just a fabrication, designed to keep us trapped?

Lena looked over at me, her expression a mix of disbelief and fear. "Dr. Cole... what if... what if she's right?"

"No," I whispered, my voice barely audible. "No, she can't be."

But even as I said the words, I could feel the foundations of my worldview cracking, crumbling beneath the weight of a truth too enormous to comprehend. The Earth... no boundaries. No space. No universe beyond what we had been shown.

I looked back at Sarah, her face calm and composed, and in that moment, I felt the ground give way beneath me.

Everything I thought I knew was a lie.

A World Under Control

The air in the village was stifling, pressing down on me with a weight I could barely comprehend. I still couldn't shake the hollow feeling in my chest after everything Sarah had revealed—about the Earth, the Controllers, the firmament. The sheer impossibility of it all rattled through my mind like a storm, and no matter how hard I tried to hold on to what I thought I knew, it was slipping away. But there was no time to process, no time to breathe. The village's quiet oppression was only the beginning. Sarah had insisted that we couldn't fully understand what we were up against—what Area 52 truly was—until we saw it with our own eyes. And so, we prepared to leave the village. Lena was pacing, glancing between me and Sarah, her face pale but her determination evident. "So, what exactly are we going to see out there?" she asked, pulling her hair back into a tight ponytail. Her voice was shaky, but she was trying to keep it steady. "I need to know what we're getting ourselves into." Sarah stood near the entrance to the stone building, watching us with a mixture of sadness and resolve. "You're going to see the truth," . "You'll see how the Reptilians have turned this land into a prison. You'll see what we've been fighting against." The chieftain, who had remained silent throughout most of the discussion, stepped forward and spoke in his guttural language. Sarah nodded and translated. "He says you need to understand that leaving the village isn't safe. The Reptilians patrol the outer regions. They watch us constantly. If they see you, they will know you're not from here." I nodded, feeling the heavy weight of the task ahead settle on my shoulders. "What do they look like?" I asked, my voice hollow. Sarah's expression darkened. "They can look like anything. Anyone. They're shape-shifters. They change their form to blend in with whatever human race they need to control. But... they can't disguise their eyes. Their real eyes. If you're close enough, you'll see them. They're... reptilian. Cold. Inhuman." Lena crossed her arms, a skeptical frown on her face. "Okay, so we're going into an area controlled by shape-shifters who can pass as human. Sounds great." I looked at her, my mind still racing with everything we'd learned. "We don't have a choice. We need to see this for ourselves." The cold stone walls of the room seemed to close in around me as we prepared for what was next. The village had been a small bubble of strange, stifling oppression, but stepping outside meant walking directly into the heart of the Reptilian-controlled area. And for that, Sarah had told us, we couldn't look like outsiders. She stood by a wooden chest at the corner of the room, pulling out dark, heavy robes and sets of small, eerie contact lenses—black lenses that would cover the whites of our eyes and mask any trace of humanity in our gaze. "You'll need to wear these," she said, her voice steady as she handed the lenses to Lena and me. "The Reptilians won't recognize you if you wear their cloaks and hide your eyes. They've kept these uniforms for secret missions, and we've used them before to infiltrate their outposts." Lena held the lenses up to the dim light, her expression uneasy. "I've worn contacts before, but... these look creepy as hell." "They're necessary," . "The Reptilians may be able to change their appearance, but their eyes are always... different. If they look into yours and see anything human, they'll know something's wrong." I stared at the black lenses in my palm, feeling the weight of the situation pressing down on me. "So, if we pass as them, we'll be able to move freely?" "For the most part," Sarah said, turning toward the bundles of clothes she had laid out. "But don't draw attention to yourselves. Reptilians are suspicious by nature, and any strange behavior could give you away. Stay close, keep your heads down, and act like you belong." Lena shot me a look. "So, just like sneaking into a government building without a clearance badge. Got it." I managed a grim smile. "Exactly." We donned the robes, their material heavier than I expected, with a strange synthetic texture that felt almost alive against my skin. The hoods draped over our heads, casting deep shadows across our faces. Once the robes were secured, I carefully placed the black lenses over my eyes. The world grew darker, and when I looked in the cracked mirror, I barely recognized myself. My eyes were black and hollow, like the Reptilian overseers we had seen watching the green-skinned workers. Lena adjusted her hood, her own eyes now hidden beneath the lenses. She looked at me, her expression unreadable behind the disguise. "Do I look terrifying enough?" she asked, her voice light but strained. "You'll blend in," Sarah assured her, already wearing her own cloak. "Now, let's move. We need to see what's happening in Area 52, and you need to understand the full scale of what we're up against." The moment we stepped out of the village and into the expanse of Area 52, the scale of the place hit me like a wave. It was like nothing I'd ever seen—like something out of a dystopian future that we, as humans, could barely dream of achieving. Towering structures made of sleek, gleaming metal rose up on the horizon, their surfaces covered in strange glyphs and glowing lines of energy. Hovering drones patrolled the skies, their mechanical eyes scanning the area below with a cold, dispassionate precision. The ground itself seemed to hum with energy. Beneath the cracked, barren earth, I could see pulses of light—strange grids of power running through the ground like veins of electricity, connecting the buildings and fueling whatever dark machinery the Reptilians used to control this land. "Keep close, " Sarah whispered, pulling her hood lower over her face as we approached a massive industrial complex. "They won't notice us if we stay quiet." As we moved closer, I could see the Reptilian patrols—hulking figures in dark robes, their heads covered by metallic helmets that masked their features. They moved with a cold, methodical precision, their eyes—those unmistakable, reptilian eyes—scanning the area constantly, searching for anything out of place. My heart pounded as we walked past them, their towering forms just inches away. My eyes stayed down, focused on the ground, but I could feel their gaze brushing over us. One wrong move, one mistake, and they would know. They would know we didn't belong. I could hear the low hum of the Reptilian machinery—massive, futuristic machines that dwarfed any technology I had seen back home. They were sleek, silent behemoths, working without pause, controlled by some unknown force. Conveyor belts moved endless lines of materials—metal, stone, glowing crystals—into towering factories that seemed to stretch into the sky itself. "This is incredible," I muttered under my breath, trying to keep my voice low. "Their technology... it's like something out of a science fiction movie." "It's far beyond anything humanity has,. "They've had this technology for centuries, long before humans were even aware of electricity. The Controllers gave it to them, allowing them to dominate their areas and keep the rest of us under control." Lena was silent, her gaze darting around, taking in everything. The sheer scale of it was overwhelming. This wasn't just a factory. This was an entire world—an empire, built on the backs of enslaved people. We passed groups of green-skinned workers, their faces expressionless, their eyes hollow as they labored under the oppressive gaze of the Reptilian overseers. There were hundreds of them, all moving in perfect synchronization, lifting heavy loads, operating advanced machinery they clearly didn't understand. It was a brutal, mechanical system, devoid of any humanity. "Is this what you've been living with for five years?" Lena asked, her voice barely a whisper. Sarah nodded. "Yes. This is what they do. They strip the land of resources, using the people as little more than tools. If you step out of line, if you resist, they take you. They... reprogram you. Change you." My fists clenched under the robes. "How have they kept this hidden for so long? Why doesn't the world know about this?" "Because of the ice walls," "The Controllers built them centuries ago, isolating each area. They control everything. They control what your governments know, what your scientists believe. No one has crossed the ice walls in over a hundred years." "But you crossed them, didn't you?" Sarah's eyes darkened, and for the first time since we'd arrived, I saw a flicker of pain in her gaze. "Yes," "I was sent here on a secret mission." We moved behind a row of large containers, hidden from view, as Sarah spoke. Her voice was low, steady, but I could hear the weight of her past in every word. "I worked for NASA," "I was an astronaut. I trained for years, but I never went to space. I never left Earth. Instead, I was chosen for a different kind of mission—one that very few people know about." Lena's eyes widened. "Wait—NASA sent you here? Beyond the ice walls?" Sarah nodded, her face pale in the dim light. "Yes. It was a secret mission, sanctioned by the U.S. government. We were sent to explore the areas beyond the ice walls, to find out what the Controllers were hiding. I was part of a team—six of us. We were told there were other areas, other civilizations, and we needed to gather information." I felt my pulse quicken. "But... you never came back." Sarah's expression tightened. "No. We were captured. The Reptilians found us as soon as we crossed into Area 52. They killed the others, but I... I was spared. They kept me here, in this village. They wanted to know why NASA had broken the deal." "Deal?" "Yes," . "NASA had an understanding with the Controllers. No one was supposed to cross the ice walls. No one was supposed to know the truth about the different areas. But my mission... it broke that agreement. And now they've been watching, waiting to see if more would come." She looked at me, her eyes narrowing slightly. "Which brings me to you. How did you get here? Did NASA send you like they sent me?" I froze, her question hanging in the air like a loaded weapon. I could feel Lena's gaze on me, waiting for my answer, but I didn't know what to say. Should I tell her the truth? That we hadn't been sent by NASA at all—that I had opened the Stargate by accident, driven by my own obsession? Or should I lie, keep the truth hidden until we knew more? "I..." I began, my voice faltering. Lena shifted beside me, her eyes hard. "Dr. Cole, now's not the time to be cryptic." I swallowed hard, avoiding Sarah's piercing gaze. "We... weren't sent by NASA," I said finally, the words tasting bitter on my tongue. "We found our way here through... different means." Sarah's eyes widened slightly, and I could see the confusion flicker across her face. "Then how did you get here?" "We used a Stargate," Lena said bluntly. "He built it. At least... that's what he's been working on." I shot her a sharp glance, but she didn't flinch. Sarah's expression darkened. "A Stargate? You... opened one?" "Yes," I admitted reluctantly. "I've been working on it for years. I never expected it to bring us here."

For a long moment, Sarah said nothing. Then, she nodded slowly, as if piecing together some unseen puzzle. "It makes sense now. The Controllers have been worried about something like this. They knew there were people on the outside—people like you—who could find a way in." Lena stepped closer, her voice firm. "So, what do we do now? How do we help?" Sarah looked at us, her eyes filled with a mix of hope and fear. "You help by doing what they fear the most. You disrupt the system. You fight back."

The farther we moved from the village, the more surreal the landscape became. Sarah led us through a winding path of broken earth and metallic ruins, her pace quick and sure, but her eyes always scanning the horizon for signs of danger. My heartbeat echoed in my ears, the weight of the disguise heavy on my shoulders, but my curiosity drove me forward. I needed to understand this place.

"This is what Area 52 looks like," I muttered, my voice barely audible under the weight of the reality around me.

Sarah turned slightly, her dark hood casting shadows across her face. "Yes. This area is divided between small, scattered villages where the green race lives, and the cities where the Reptilians control everything."

We passed through more barren land, the cracked ground giving way to strange, pulsing energy grids that seemed to light the way toward the towering cities in the distance. The contrast between the desolate villages and the high-tech cities was impossible to miss.

I could see one such city now—dark, monolithic towers piercing the sky, connected by glowing bridges of light and mechanical arms that stretched out like fingers, weaving between the buildings. Strange aerial crafts buzzed around the city like insects, hovering over the intricate web of technology that made up the Reptilian world. It was more advanced than anything I'd ever seen, far beyond human technology.

Lena, her hood pulled low over her blackened eyes, whispered next to me. "This place... it's like something out of a nightmare. How could they keep this hidden?"

"They've been controlling it all for centuries," Sarah answered softly, glancing toward the distant city. "They have ways of ensuring no one outside the ice walls knows the truth. The Controllers isolated each region with those boundaries, and no one has been able to cross. The Reptilians rule over Area 52, and this is the world they've created. Villages where the green race serves, and cities where the Reptilians reign, wielding technology we can barely comprehend."

Lena nodded grimly, her eyes darting from the towering structures to the beaten-down green-skinned workers trudging across the landscape. "So, the villages... they're just used for labor?"

"Yes," Sarah replied, her voice tense. "They extract resources from the land, building their cities, strengthening their hold. Every village has its role—some work the fields, some build weapons, others mine for rare minerals. The Reptilians never let the villagers near their cities. That's where they keep their technology, and that's where they maintain their control."

I stared at the city in the distance, my mind spinning. "You said Area 52 is the same size as Area 51?"

Sarah nodded. "That's what I've been told. Area 52 stretches far beyond what you've seen here. It's vast, divided into different regions, much like Area 51. But here... the Reptilians control everything. They monitor every village, every movement. The technology they use is designed to keep the people under their thumb, to make sure no one tries to rebel."

I took a deep breath, my eyes tracing the massive structures ahead of us. The gleaming towers, the alien machines—it was all so far beyond what I'd ever imagined. "And no one's ever been able to escape?"

Sarah shook her head. "We've tried. Many have tried. The green-skinned people have staged surprise revolts, but every time they rise up, they're crushed by the Reptilians' advanced technology. Their weapons are too powerful, their surveillance too vast. And when someone defies them... they disappear. No one comes back."

The weight of her words settled on me like a stone, the grim reality of this place pressing in from all sides. This wasn't just about science, about understanding the universe. This was about survival—about breaking free from a system of control that had been in place for centuries. But could we help? Could our knowledge really make a difference against an enemy so far beyond anything we'd ever faced?

Lena's voice cut through my thoughts. "So what now? We just keep moving and hope they don't notice us?"

Sarah nodded, her eyes scanning the horizon again. "We need to stay out of sight. The Reptilian patrols are everywhere. If they find us—"

She stopped abruptly, her body going rigid.

I followed her gaze and felt my stomach drop.

The Reptilian Patrol

In the distance, closing in fast, was a **Reptilian patrol**—a group of four figures, tall and imposing, their dark cloaks billowing as they moved with swift, purposeful strides. Their cold, reptilian eyes gleamed under the dim light, scanning the area with a precision that made my blood run cold.

"They're coming this way," Lena whispered, her voice tight with fear.

Sarah's expression darkened. "Stay calm. Keep your hoods up and your eyes low. If they think you're one of them, they'll pass right by."

We nodded, falling into step behind Sarah as she continued to lead us down the path. My heart pounded in my chest, each beat louder than the last as the patrol drew closer. The wind seemed to still, the air growing heavier with every step.

They were close now. Too close.

I kept my eyes down, my hood low, but I could feel their presence like a weight pressing against my chest. The ground beneath my feet seemed to vibrate with the hum of their technology, the air around us thick with tension. We walked in silence, our footsteps barely making a sound as we passed through the shadow of the towering city.

But then, the Reptilians stopped.

My breath caught in my throat. I could hear the soft murmur of their voices—low, hissing sounds that sent a chill down my spine. One of them stepped forward, his eyes narrowing as he turned toward us, suspicion etched across his reptilian features.

I dared not look up, my hands trembling beneath the cloak. If they saw through our disguise, if they realized who we really were...

Sarah's voice was calm but firm. "Don't react. Keep moving."

We kept walking, our pace steady, but the Reptilian who had stepped forward wasn't moving. His eyes were fixed on us, and I could feel the scrutiny in his gaze, sharp and calculating.

"Something's not right," Lena whispered, barely audible.

Suddenly, the Reptilian patrol leader spoke in a guttural, alien tongue—a command. His voice was cold, dripping with authority.

"They've seen us," Sarah hissed under her breath. "Don't stop. Don't—"

But it was too late. The patrol surged forward, their heavy steps thundering against the ground, their cloaks billowing like dark storm clouds. The leader grabbed my arm, his grip like iron, and wrenched me toward him. I stumbled, my hood falling back slightly, and for a brief moment, our eyes met.

I saw it in his gaze—recognition. He knew. He knew we didn't belong.

A sickening sense of dread washed over me as the Reptilian leader barked another command. His hand tightened around my arm, and I could feel the raw strength in his grip. This wasn't just a warning. They were taking us.

Lena gasped, trying to pull away from one of the Reptilians who had grabbed her, but it was no use. Their strength was overwhelming. They moved with the precision of soldiers, their cold eyes gleaming with triumph as they dragged us toward their waiting vehicle.

Panic surged in my chest. "Sarah!" I shouted, my voice cracking.

Sarah tried to resist, but she was quickly overpowered. "We've been compromised," she gasped, her voice tight with fear. "They know. They—"

Before she could finish, the Reptilian leader pulled something from his cloak—a sleek, metallic device—and pressed it against my neck. I felt a sharp sting, followed by a wave of darkness washing over my senses. My body went limp, and I fell to the ground, my vision fading.

The last thing I heard before everything went black was Lena's voice, a single, terrified cry echoing through the air.

The Awakening

My mind felt like it was floating, disconnected from my body as if it had been severed from the physical world and left adrift in a void. Slowly, like a rising tide, awareness returned to me, trickling in with flashes of memory—fragments of the Reptilian patrol, the blinding lights, and the overwhelming strength that had pinned me down. My body was stiff, restrained, but I couldn't yet open my eyes.

Lena's voice, soft but strained, broke through the fog.

"Dr. Cole... Ethan, can you hear me?"

The mention of my name snapped something into place, and my eyes shot open. My vision blurred momentarily, adjusting to the sterile, harsh lighting that filled the room. Cold. Clinical. Everything was made of sleek, metal-like surfaces, but none that I could immediately recognize. The walls gleamed with a glassy sheen, reflecting a subtle glow that pulsed from thin strips of light embedded in the ceiling.

I turned my head toward the sound of Lena's voice. She sat a few feet away, slumped against the wall, her wrists shackled in front of her, just like mine. Her face was pale, streaked with dried blood from a cut near her temple. She was trying to free herself from the metallic restraints around her wrists but with no success.

"Lena," I croaked, my throat dry and raw. "Where are we?"

"I don't know," she whispered, her voice trembling slightly. "One minute we were in the village, and the next... I remember those Reptilians grabbing us, and then nothing."

I tried to sit up, only to realize that I was also shackled, my arms held tightly by the cold metal. I glanced around the room, my scientist's mind kicking in automatically, assessing our environment.

The cell was large but stark, every surface gleaming with a sterile, almost alien cleanliness. One wall wasn't a wall at all but a transparent barrier that acted like glass, though I doubted it was anything so primitive. Beyond it, I could see a hallway illuminated by that same harsh lighting. Every now and then, strange, spherical drones—about the size of a basketball—floated past, scanning the hallway with beams of light that swept from left to right, searching for any signs of disturbance.

"We need to get out of here," Lena said, panic beginning to edge into her voice. "What if they—what if they've already—"

"We're not dead yet," I said, trying to sound calm, though my heart was hammering in my chest. "If they wanted us dead, they would've killed us back in the village."

"Then what do they want with us?"

"I don't know," I replied, my voice tight. "But we need to figure it out."

I shifted my body, testing the strength of the restraints around my wrists. They were firm, and the material was cold to the touch, but it wasn't metallic. It was something else, something smoother, and when I tugged at it, the band seemed to hum slightly, like a living thing.

Lena noticed it too. "What is this? Some kind of material?"

I squinted at the bands. "Nanotechnology, maybe? Something that responds to pressure. But it's unlike anything I've ever seen."

My scientific curiosity surged through the fog of fear, momentarily taking over. I began to study the room with more interest. The transparent barrier intrigued me. It wasn't glass, but it looked like it had the properties of glass—clear, smooth, yet strangely resilient. My gaze drifted outside the barrier again, and for the first time, I noticed that we weren't the only ones trapped.

Figures moved beyond the glass, some human, others with the pale green skin of the people we had encountered in the village. They were being led down the hallway in single file, their heads bowed, their eyes hollow. Occasionally, one would be pulled out of the line and escorted through a door I couldn't see. But what disturbed me most was how they moved—like they were lifeless, their bodies shuffling as if they were barely conscious.

Lena's eyes followed mine, widening. "What are they doing to them?"

"I don't know," I said, though the hairs on the back of my neck were standing on end. "But it looks like they're being processed."

"Processed? What does that even mean?"

"I don't know," I repeated, more to myself than to her.

We both sat in silence for a moment, the weight of our situation pressing down on us. My thoughts raced, flipping between panic and logic. Where was Sarah? Was she in another cell, or had she been taken somewhere else? And if she had... what were they doing to her?

"Sarah..." Lena whispered, echoing my thoughts. "Do you think... do you think she's alive?"

I hesitated, not wanting to vocalize my own fear. "I hope so."

"But what if she's—"

"Don't," I said sharply, cutting her off. "Don't go there. Not yet."

Lena fell silent, her eyes filled with worry and exhaustion.

Suddenly, a voice, low and raspy, cut through the silence. It came from the cell next to ours, though I couldn't see the speaker.

"You're wasting your time," the voice said. "The Reptilians don't care about your struggles. The moment they bring you in, you're theirs."

Lena and I exchanged a glance, startled.

"Who's there?" I called out.

A figure moved into view on the other side of the transparent barrier between cells. It was an older man, his skin pale and gaunt, his eyes sunken. His wrists were bound in the same way ours were, and there was a haunted look in his eyes.

"You're new here," he said, almost as if it were a fact, not a question.

"Who are you?" I asked, leaning forward as much as my restraints would allow.

"It doesn't matter who I am," he said, his voice hollow. "What matters is what they're going to do to you. You won't survive the interrogation."

Lena's face paled. "What interrogation?"

The man's expression darkened. "They'll take you soon. One by one. They'll use their machines to dig into your mind, pull out your deepest memories, your darkest secrets. You won't be able to resist it. None of us can."

I felt a cold dread creep down my spine. "Mind control?"

"Worse than that," the man said quietly. "They can rewrite your mind, erase everything you know. And when they're done with you, you'll be like them." He gestured toward the figures being led down the hallway. "Empty. Hollow. You'll become part of their machine."

Lena's breath hitched, her eyes widening in fear. "No... they wouldn't..."

"Believe me, they will," the man said, his voice tinged with bitterness. "They've done it to everyone here."

I shook my head, trying to keep my grip on rational thought. "There must be a way to escape."

"Escape?" The man gave a bitter laugh. "There's no escape. You're in their world now. No one escapes."

Just then, the sound of footsteps echoed down the hallway, and Lena stiffened. A group of Reptilian guards appeared, their tall, imposing figures moving with mechanical precision. One of them approached a neighboring cell, where a woman was sitting, her head bowed. Without a word, the Reptilian pressed a panel on the wall, and the barrier around her cell vanished. Two guards grabbed her by the arms, pulling her to her feet. She didn't resist. She didn't even scream. She was completely numb, devoid of any fight.

But as they dragged her away, her lifeless eyes briefly met mine, and I saw the flicker of something in them. Fear. Desperation. But it was too late. The guards disappeared down the hallway with her, the sound of their footsteps fading into the distance.

Lena's hands were shaking. "Did you see that? Did you—"

Her voice was cut off by the distant sound of a scream. It was sharp, filled with agony... and then it stopped. The silence that followed was deafening.

The man in the next cell spoke again, his voice lower now. "That's what happens when they take you for 'processing.' Once you're gone, you're never the same again."

Lena looked at me, her face pale. "What do we do, Ethan? What if they take us next? What if... what if we don't make it out?"

I wished I had an answer, but the truth was, I didn't know. I had no idea what we were up against, or how we could fight back. My mind raced with a thousand possible escape plans, but each one seemed more futile than the last.

"We'll find a way," I said finally, though my voice lacked conviction. "We'll figure something out."

Lena didn't look convinced, and frankly, neither was I.

But before we could say anything more, the sound of footsteps echoed down the hallway again, this time stopping directly in front of our cell. I looked up, my heart pounding, as a pair of Reptilian guards appeared outside the transparent barrier, their eyes cold and calculating.

Without a word, one of them pressed a panel on the wall, and the barrier separating us from the hallway disappeared. The other guard stepped inside, towering over us with a menacing presence.

"Get up," he growled in a guttural voice.

Lena and I exchanged a terrified glance.

It was our turn.

Interrogation

I couldn't breathe. My feet stumbled over the cold, metallic floor as the Reptilian guard shoved me forward, the hard grip of his hand like iron clamped around my arm. My mind raced, the tension building with every step as we approached the looming door at the end of the long, sterile corridor. I glanced to the side, but Lena was no longer beside me. They had separated us as soon as we left the cell.

I could still hear the echoes of Lena's panicked breathing when they had dragged her in the opposite direction. My heart pounded against my ribs, the dread twisting tighter around my chest.

"Where are you taking her?" I'd demanded, but the guards didn't bother to answer.

The hallway stretched on forever, the bright lights reflecting off the smooth, gleaming walls. My eyes darted around, catching brief glimpses of other captives through the translucent barriers lining the corridor. Human. Green-skinned. All broken, empty, and lost.

The door ahead slid open with a cold hiss, and the Reptilian guard practically threw me inside. I stumbled forward and caught myself on a steel chair bolted to the floor. The room was small, barren, and terrifyingly cold—so cold that my breath misted in the air in front of me. A thick, glass-like wall stretched across the far side of the room, revealing a control station on the other side, where I could make out vague, shadowy figures monitoring the room's activity.

Without a word, the Reptilian pushed me into the chair and strapped my arms and legs to it. The restraints tightened painfully around my wrists and ankles. I was trapped.

My head spun as I tried to make sense of everything. Where was Lena? What had they done to her? And what were they planning to do to me?

The Reptilian guard loomed over me, his yellow eyes cold and unblinking as he inspected the restraints. His skin, mottled and rough like a snake's, caught the light from the overhead bulbs, making him look even more alien than I could have imagined.

"Why are you doing this?" I asked, my voice hoarse.

He didn't respond.

Suddenly, a loud hum filled the room, and I felt something shift in the air. I looked up to see that the glass-like wall had changed, revealing more of the shadowy figures beyond. This time, I could make out three distinct figures standing in the control room. One of them stepped closer to the glass.

My breath caught in my throat.

It was **Sarah**.

My heart dropped into my stomach. She was alive—but that relief was quickly washed away by a surge of confusion. She was standing with the Reptilians, dressed in a sleek, dark uniform that I had never seen her wear before. Her face was expressionless, cold, almost as if she didn't recognize me.

"Sarah?" I gasped, my voice cracking.

Her eyes met mine, but there was no recognition there—just the same cold indifference that I had seen in the Reptilians.

"Sarah, what the hell is going on?" I demanded, my voice shaking.

She didn't answer. Instead, one of the Reptilians in the control room leaned closer to her and whispered something in her ear. She nodded mechanically and stepped toward the glass, her gaze still fixed on me.

I felt a rush of anger and disbelief. "You're working with them? Sarah, why? We trusted you!"

The room felt like it was closing in on me. My breath quickened, my chest tightening with a flood of emotions. Fear, anger, betrayal—it all swirled together in a chaotic storm inside me.

Sarah stepped closer, her face still devoid of emotion. "Ethan," she said finally, her voice calm, almost soothing. "You don't understand. I had no choice."

"No choice? What do you mean, no choice?" I snapped, struggling against the restraints. "We trusted you! You were with us! What are you doing here?"

"They know everything, Ethan," Sarah continued, her voice eerily calm. "They've known for a long time. About NASA. About the Stargate. About the project."

A cold shiver ran down my spine.

Lena had been right. The Reptilians knew far more than we ever imagined. It was as if they had been watching us—monitoring us—this entire time.

"They know about the Stargate?" I repeated, my voice barely more than a whisper. "How? How could they possibly know?"

Sarah glanced at the Reptilian next to her, who nodded in approval. Then she turned back to me, her eyes hardening. "You were never alone, Ethan. The Controllers have been watching you for years. They knew about the project before you even began."

I stared at her, my mind reeling. "That's impossible. We worked in complete secrecy—no one outside of NASA knew about it."

"You were wrong," Sarah said simply, her voice icy. "Everything you've done—everything you've worked for—was orchestrated by them. They wanted to understand how the human mind in Area 51 could evolve. They monitored you: your project, your failures, your breakthroughs. They let you believe you were in control, but you never were."

The room tilted around me. I felt like I was drowning in disbelief. "This... this can't be real."

"It's real," Sarah said, her voice unwavering. "The Controllers have been waiting for you to open the Stargate. They knew it was only a matter of time before you succeeded. You've triggered something bigger than you realize."

Lena's words from earlier echoed in my mind: *How do they know all of this?* It was impossible. It didn't make any sense.

"And now," Sarah added coldly, "they want to know more."

My heart pounded in my chest as I processed her words. The Reptilians—no, the Controllers—they had been behind everything. They had let us stumble around in the dark, playing with technology we didn't fully understand, only to pull the strings when it suited them.

"Sarah," I whispered, my voice hoarse with desperation, "you don't have to do this. You're one of us. You can still help us."

But Sarah's face remained emotionless. "It's too late for that," she said softly. "There's no escaping them. Not for me. Not for you."

Before I could respond, the hum of machinery filled the room once again, louder this time. I felt something clamp down around my head—a cold, metallic band that I hadn't noticed before. It hummed with energy, and I could feel it vibrating against my skull.

"What... what is this?" I gasped, struggling against the restraints.

Sarah watched me with detached indifference. "This is where they learn everything."

A flash of bright light exploded behind my eyes, and suddenly I was no longer in the sterile room. I was in my childhood home—my father's study. The familiar scent of old books and leather filled my senses, and I could hear the ticking of the grandfather clock in the corner. Everything felt so vivid, so real.

But it wasn't real.

I knew it wasn't.

And yet... standing in front of me, leaning over the desk with a warm smile, was my father. He looked just as he had before he died—strong, confident, his eyes filled with wisdom.

"Ethan," he said, his voice gentle, "it's good to see you, son."

My heart clenched painfully in my chest. My father. God, it had been years since I'd heard his voice. He looked so real. So alive.

"Dad?" I whispered, my voice breaking.

"It's okay," he said, stepping around the desk to stand in front of me. "You don't need to fight anymore, son. Just let go. Let them help you."

I blinked rapidly, trying to shake the illusion, but it was so real. I could feel the warmth of the room, hear the crackle of the fire in the hearth.

"Let them help you," my father repeated, his voice soft and comforting. "You've done enough. It's time to let go."

"No," I whispered, shaking my head. "No, this isn't real. You're not real."

But his hand reached out, warm and solid, resting on my shoulder. "It's all right, Ethan. You've done your part. You don't have to fight anymore."

I felt myself wavering, my mind splitting between the real and the illusion. It was so tempting to believe him, to give in to the warmth and comfort of his presence. But deep down, I knew it was a lie.

This wasn't my father. This was the Reptilians.

They were playing with my mind.

"No!" I shouted, wrenching myself away from the illusion.

The warmth of the study vanished in an instant, replaced by the cold, sterile reality of the interrogation room. My head throbbed painfully, and I gasped for breath, feeling the metal band hum against my skull.

Sarah watched me with an unreadable expression, but there was a flicker of something in her eyes—something almost human.

Before I could say anything, the door to the interrogation room slid open, and another Reptilian guard stepped inside.

"'Take him back to his cell,' the guard's voice echoed in my mind, and I understood every word."

As the restraints around my arms and legs were released, I slumped forward, my body weak and trembling. The Reptilian guard hauled me to my feet and dragged me toward the door.

But just before we reached the exit, I glanced back at Sarah one last time.

"Why?" I asked, my voice barely audible. "Why are you doing this?"

She didn't answer.

The door slid shut behind me with a cold hiss, leaving me alone with my thoughts—and the unbearable weight of betrayal.

A Moment of Chaos

I was dragged down the hallway, my body barely able to keep up with the Reptilian guard's harsh pace. My legs felt weak, like jelly, and my mind was reeling from what I had just experienced. The image of my father was still fresh in my head, vivid and warm, as if I could still hear his voice echoing through my mind.

But it wasn't real. It couldn't have been real.

Just let go...

No. I couldn't. There was too much at stake—too many unanswered questions, too many dangers that lay ahead. And Sarah—God, Sarah. Was she really working with them? Or was this some kind of elaborate manipulation? I could hardly believe it, but there she was, cold and distant, standing side by side with the Reptilians like one of them.

Why would she betray us like this?

The Reptilian guard gave my arm a violent yank, snapping me out of my spiraling thoughts. I glanced up, the cold lights reflecting off the smooth walls, giving the hallway an eerie glow. The air was frigid, sterile. Somewhere far off, I could hear the faint hum of machinery, and every so often, the soft whoosh of doors opening and closing in the distance.

We passed by several cells, each one filled with captives—some human, some green-skinned. Their eyes were hollow, their expressions lifeless, and as we moved past, I couldn't help but wonder how long they'd been here. Had they undergone the same interrogation? The same manipulation? Were they already lost, their minds broken by the Reptilians?

I clenched my fists, trying to push away the rising fear. *I'm not like them,* I told myself. *I'll find a way out of this.*

But every step I took, every second that passed, brought me deeper into the belly of the beast. Deeper into whatever hellish fate awaited us.

Suddenly, the guard came to an abrupt stop in front of a door, its sleek surface gleaming under the harsh light. Without a word, the guard pressed his hand against a panel on the wall, and the door slid open with a soft hiss. I was shoved inside, the door closing behind me with a finality that made my stomach churn.

The room was small, cold, and clinical. It was similar to the one I had been interrogated in, but there was something different about this one—something more ominous. A metallic chair sat in the center of the room, equipped with restraints for both the arms and legs. Overhead, strange machines and monitors lined the ceiling, their screens flickering with symbols and data that I couldn't decipher. The walls were bare, save for the glass-like panel that separated this room from the control station on the other side.

And there, seated on a raised platform behind the glass, were two Reptilian figures—watching. Waiting.

I swallowed hard as the guard shoved me toward the chair. "Sit," he commanded, his voice a guttural growl.

Reluctantly, I lowered myself into the chair, the cold metal biting into my skin. The restraints automatically snapped into place around my wrists and ankles, locking me in. I was trapped. Again.

The guard stepped back, watching me with those cold, reptilian eyes, before turning to leave the room. The door slid shut behind him, and I was left alone—alone with the cold silence, the flashing screens, and the eerie presence of the Reptilian overseers behind the glass.

I tried to steady my breathing, to think clearly. There had to be a way out of this. But the truth was, I had no idea what they were going to do to me next. They had already dug into my mind, pulled out pieces of my past, used it against me. What more could they want?

I was about to find out.

Without warning, the monitors above me flickered to life. Strange symbols and patterns flashed across the screens, and a low hum filled the room. I felt a sudden pressure on my head, and then... nothing.

Everything went black.

When I opened my eyes, I wasn't in the cold, sterile room anymore. I was... somewhere else. Somewhere familiar.

I stood in the middle of a vast, open field, the sky overhead a brilliant shade of blue. The sun shone brightly, casting warm rays over the tall grass that swayed gently in the breeze. Birds chirped in the distance, and the sweet smell of wildflowers filled the air.

I knew this place. I had been here before.

It was the field behind my childhood home.

For a moment, I stood there, frozen, taking in the scene. It was so real—so vivid. I could feel the warmth of the sun on my skin, the soft rustle of the wind in the grass. Everything about it felt real.

But it wasn't real. I knew that. This was the Reptilians' doing. Another mind game.

But even as I tried to ground myself in reality, something inside me wavered. It was so tempting to believe—to give in to the illusion. To lose myself in the comfort of the past.

As I stood there, staring out at the horizon, I heard a voice behind me. A voice that sent a jolt of shock through my entire body.

"Ethan."

I turned around slowly, my heart hammering in my chest.

Standing there, just a few feet away from me, was my father. His dark hair was flecked with gray, just as I remembered, and his eyes held that same warm, knowing expression that had always made me feel safe. He smiled at me, a soft, gentle smile, the kind that made me feel like everything was going to be okay.

"Dad?" I whispered, my voice trembling.

He took a step closer, his hands outstretched, as if inviting me into an embrace. "It's me, son."

"No," I muttered, shaking my head. "No, you're not real. You're not—"

"Ethan," he said again, his voice soft and soothing. "I know you're scared. I know you don't understand what's happening. But you don't have to fight anymore. It's okay to let go."

I took a step back, my mind reeling. This wasn't real. It couldn't be. My father had been dead for years. But the way he looked at me, the way he spoke—it was so convincing. So real.

"I'm not giving up," I said, my voice shaking. "I'm not letting them win."

My father smiled again, a sad, knowing smile. "You don't have to fight them, Ethan. They're not your enemy. They're trying to help you. All you have to do is trust them."

I shook my head violently. "No. No, this is a lie. You're not my father. You're just a figment of my mind—something they created to manipulate me."

"Ethan," he said softly, stepping closer, "it's okay. I'm here. You don't have to be afraid."

"Stop!" I shouted, my voice cracking. "Stop it!"

But he kept coming closer, his arms outstretched, his eyes filled with that same warm, loving expression. I stumbled back, my heart racing, my breath coming in ragged gasps.

"I'm not giving up," I repeated, more to myself than to him. "I'm not giving up."

He stopped just a few feet away from me, his expression softening. "I'm proud of you, son. You've done so much. But it's time to let go. It's time to come home."

The tears welled up in my eyes, unbidden and unwanted. I tried to blink them away, but they wouldn't stop. My chest heaved with the effort of holding back the sobs that threatened to break free.

But I couldn't give in. I wouldn't give in.

"Dad..." I whispered, my voice trembling with emotion. "I miss you. God, I miss you so much."

"I know," he said, his voice filled with warmth. "I miss you too, Ethan."

"I can't..." I choked, my throat tight with emotion. "I can't let them win."

He smiled again, that same sad smile. "It's okay. You've done your part. Now it's time to rest."

I closed my eyes, fighting against the wave of emotion that surged through me. It would be so easy to give in—to let go and fall into the comforting embrace of my father. But deep down, I knew that this wasn't real. It was just another trick—another manipulation.

"I'm not giving up," I said again, my voice stronger this time. "I'm not letting them win."

When I opened my eyes, my father was gone.

The warmth of the sun vanished, replaced by the cold, sterile air of the interrogation room. My body jerked as I came back to reality, my heart racing, my breath coming in ragged gasps. I was still strapped to the chair, the restraints digging into my wrists and ankles. The metal band around my head hummed faintly, sending a dull throb of pain through my skull.

But I had resisted. I hadn't given in.

The Reptilian figures behind the glass watched me with cold, calculating eyes. One of them leaned closer to the control panel, his scaled fingers dancing over the buttons and levers.

The door slid open, and the guard who had brought me here stepped inside. His eyes glinted with something dark, something that made my skin crawl.

"Take him back to his cell," one of the Reptilians behind the glass commanded in a low, guttural voice.

The guard grabbed me by the arm and yanked me to my feet, my legs barely able to support my weight. My mind was still reeling from the illusion, the emotional manipulation, the vividness of my father's voice.

As the guard dragged me toward the door, I cast one last glance at the Reptilians behind the glass. Their cold, unfeeling eyes met mine, and in that moment, I knew—I had only scratched the surface of what they were capable of.

The real battle had just begun.

The Great Escape

The cold metallic floor scraped against my cheek as I was dragged down the corridor, my body limp and battered. My mind struggled to focus, still reeling from the psychological torment I'd just endured. The illusion of my father, so real, so tangible, echoed in my thoughts, pulling at the seams of my sanity. But I couldn't afford to let myself fall apart. I had to stay grounded. I had to stay focused.

They'd tried to break me in that room, digging into my memories, playing with my emotions, twisting my past to make me compliant. But I hadn't given in. And I wouldn't.

The Reptilian guard's grip on my arm was like iron, his taloned fingers digging into my skin as he dragged me along the dimly lit corridor. The lights overhead flickered, casting an eerie glow on the glass-like walls that lined the passage. My legs barely functioned, and every step felt like a monumental effort, but I knew one thing for sure—I had to get back to Lena. I had to find her. She was the only thing tethering me to reality, the only thing reminding me why I had to fight.

The door to the cell came into view, the translucent surface reflecting the pale light from above. Without a word, the Reptilian guard shoved me inside, the door sliding shut behind me with a soft hiss.

I stumbled forward, my knees giving out beneath me as I collapsed to the cold floor. Pain shot up my legs, but it was nothing compared to the overwhelming sense of disorientation clouding my mind. For a moment, I just lay there, trying to gather my thoughts, trying to push through the fog that clung to my consciousness.

And then I heard her.

"Mom... is that you?"

Lena's voice was soft, trembling, and completely out of place. My heart sank as I forced myself to sit up, my eyes searching the small cell for her.

She was sitting in the far corner, her back against the wall, her knees drawn up to her chest. Her eyes were wide and unfocused, staring at something that wasn't there. Her hands trembled as she reached out toward the empty space in front of her, her lips moving in a whisper.

"Mom, I... I didn't mean to leave you. I'm sorry."

My stomach twisted into a knot as I realized what was happening. They had gotten to her too. They had broken into her mind, twisted her memories, manipulated her deepest fears and desires.

"Lena," I whispered, my voice hoarse as I crawled toward her. "Lena, it's me. It's Ethan."

She didn't respond. Her eyes remained fixed on the empty space in front of her, her hands trembling as she reached out, as though she were trying to grasp something invisible.

"Mom, please," she whimpered, her voice cracking with emotion. "Please, don't leave me again."

My heart shattered at the sound of her voice. I reached out and gently placed my hand on her shoulder, trying to shake her out of whatever hellish illusion they'd trapped her in.

"Lena, it's not real," I said softly, my voice trembling. "Whatever you're seeing, it's not real. I'm here. You're safe."

She flinched at my touch, pulling away from me as though I were some kind of ghost. Her eyes darted around the room, wild and unfocused, as she whispered to herself.

"I'm sorry... I didn't mean to... I didn't mean to leave you, Mom. I didn't..."

Her words trailed off, her voice breaking with a sob.

I felt a surge of anger rise in my chest, directed not at her but at the monsters who had done this to her—who had manipulated her mind, twisted her memories, and left her broken and confused. I clenched my fists, trying to push down the rage, trying to stay focused on the one thing that mattered right now: getting her back.

"Lena," I said again, more firmly this time, as I moved closer to her. "It's me, Ethan. I'm here. You're not alone."

For a moment, she didn't respond. Her eyes remained distant, her mind trapped in whatever illusion the Reptilians had forced on her. But slowly—so slowly—her gaze began to shift. She blinked, her brow furrowing as though she were struggling to understand where she was.

"Ethan?" she whispered, her voice barely audible.

"Yes," I said, relief flooding my chest as I reached for her hand. "I'm here. You're safe."

She blinked again, her eyes slowly focusing on me. "I... I saw my mom."

Tears welled up in her eyes, and I could see the devastation etched across her face. She looked so lost, so broken. My heart ached for her, but I didn't know how to comfort her. How could I? We were trapped in a cell, at the mercy of beings far beyond our comprehension, and her mind had just been torn apart by memories that weren't real.

"They made you see her," I said softly, squeezing her hand. "It wasn't real, Lena. It was just another one of their tricks. You have to fight it."

Her lips trembled as she nodded, her tears spilling down her cheeks. "I miss her so much."

"I know," I whispered, my own voice thick with emotion. "But we can't let them win. We have to stay strong."

She sniffed, wiping her eyes with the back of her hand. "What... what do they want from us, Ethan? Why are they doing this?"

"I don't know," I admitted, the weight of that uncertainty pressing down on me. "But whatever it is, we can't let them break us."

For a long moment, we just sat there in silence, the cold reality of our situation settling over us like a heavy fog. I could still hear the faint hum of machinery outside the cell, the soft whoosh of doors opening and closing in the distance. Every now and then, a distant scream would echo through the hallway, the sound sending chills down my spine.

Lena leaned her head against my shoulder, her body trembling with exhaustion. "Do you think… do you think Sarah is okay?"

The question hit me like a punch to the gut. I didn't know how to answer that. After everything we had seen, after the way Sarah had appeared to be working with the Reptilians, I didn't know what to think. I didn't know who to trust anymore.

"I don't know," I admitted honestly. "I really don't know what to say to you, but Sarah isn't on our side right now."

what do you mean?

Then, without warning, the sound of gunfire shattered the stillness.

Lena jerked upright, her eyes wide with fear. "What was that?"

I scrambled to my feet, my heart racing as I strained to listen. More gunshots echoed through the corridor, followed by the unmistakable sound of screams—screams that chilled my blood, like something straight out of hell itself. The noise was getting closer, the sound of chaos, of destruction.

"What the hell is going on out there?" I muttered, my voice tight with fear.

Before either of us could move, the door to our cell slid open with a hiss. Lena gasped, her hand flying to her mouth as a figure stepped through the doorway.

It was Sarah.

But something was different about her. She wasn't wearing the cold, detached expression she had in the control room. Her eyes were wide with urgency, and her face was pale, her skin slick with sweat. She looked terrified.

"Sarah?" I whispered, my voice laced with disbelief.

She didn't say anything. She just rushed toward us, her fingers flying over a small device she held in her hand. For a moment, I thought she was going to attack us, but then a faint hum filled the air, and I felt a strange shift in the atmosphere.

A swirling, shimmering portal materialized in the center of the room, its surface rippling like liquid glass. The sight of it made my stomach flip.

"The Stargate..." Lena whispered, her eyes wide with shock.

I stared at the portal, my heart racing. How the hell had she opened it? And why?

"Get up," Sarah ordered, her voice trembling with urgency. "We don't have much time."

"What the hell is going on?" I demanded, my mind spinning with questions. "How did you—"

"There's no time to explain!" she snapped, her voice rising in panic. "If we don't leave now, we're all dead."

I could hear the gunshots getting closer, the screams growing louder. Whatever was happening out there, it wasn't going to stop. And if Sarah had found a way to get us out, I wasn't going to argue.

"Come on," I said, grabbing Lena's hand and pulling her to her feet.

Sarah stepped toward the portal, her face pale but determined. "Stay close to me. I can't hold it open for long."

I didn't need to be told twice.

Together, the three of us rushed toward the swirling Stargate, the sound of chaos and destruction echoing behind us. The air around the portal crackled with energy, the light from its surface casting strange, shifting shadows across the cell walls.

I hesitated for a split second, my heart racing as I stared into the shimmering surface of the portal. We had no idea where it would take us, no idea what waited for us on the other side. But staying here was certain death.

Lena squeezed my hand, her voice trembling. "Ethan..."

"I know," I whispered, my breath catching in my throat. "We have to go."

Without another word, we stepped forward, the portal swallowing us in a flash of light.

The sensation of being pulled through the Stargate was unlike anything I had ever experienced. It was like being stretched, twisted, and folded all at once, my body and mind torn apart and reassembled in a fraction of a second. The light was blinding, the sound a deafening roar, and for a moment, I wasn't sure if I was still alive.

But then, just as quickly as it had started, the sensation stopped.

I staggered forward, gasping for breath as the world around me snapped back into focus. The cold, sterile air of the Reptilian facility was gone, replaced by the familiar sights and sounds of the village. The green-skinned villagers moved about in the distance, their eyes wide with shock as they watched us appear out of thin air.

"We made it," Lena whispered, her voice filled with disbelief. "We're back..."

I turned to Sarah, who was standing beside me, her face pale and exhausted. She looked like she had aged a decade in the last few minutes, her shoulders slumped with the weight of whatever burden she was carrying.

But there was no time for relief. No time to celebrate.

Because somewhere, deep inside the Reptilian facility, the Controllers were already regrouping. And they weren't going to stop until they found us.   Forgiveness and Revolution

The village was quiet, unnervingly so. The green-skinned villagers went about their lives with a somber, mechanical routine, as if they had long accepted the weight of their oppression. The air was heavy with tension, and the remnants of the night's terror still clung to the wind. Lena and I stood by a small fire, trying to make sense of everything that had happened. The warmth of the flames barely touched the cold knot of anxiety lodged in my chest.

Behind us, Sarah sat on a low stone bench, her face pale and drawn, her eyes fixed on the ground as though she were staring at something only she could see. She hadn't said much since we'd escaped through the Stargate, and I hadn't pressed her. Not yet.

But the questions burned in my mind. Why had she helped us? Why now, after everything she had done? And more importantly, could we trust her?

I glanced at Lena, who was sitting next to me, still recovering from the psychological torture the Reptilians had inflicted on her. She had been quiet ever since we'd arrived back at the village, her mind clearly struggling to process the illusions they had forced on her. I wanted to comfort her, to tell her everything would be okay, but how could I? I didn't even know if we'd make it out of this alive.

The fire crackled softly, and the tension in the air finally became too much to bear.

"Sarah," I said, my voice low and steady. "We need to talk."

She didn't look up, but I saw her shoulders tense. She knew this was coming. She had to.

For a moment, she didn't speak, just stared at the ground as though she were gathering her thoughts. Then, with a deep breath, she finally lifted her head and met my gaze.

"I know what you're thinking, Ethan," she said softly, her voice laced with exhaustion. "You think I betrayed you."

I crossed my arms, my jaw clenched. "You stood there with them, Sarah. You watched while they tortured us, while they tore our minds apart. How am I supposed to see that as anything other than betrayal?"

Her eyes flickered with pain, and she looked away. "You don't understand. I didn't have a choice."

"Didn't have a choice?" I repeated, my voice rising. "You *always* have a choice, Sarah."

Her gaze snapped back to mine, and for the first time since we'd returned to the village, I saw a flicker of anger in her eyes. "Do you have any idea what it's like to be trapped here? To be hunted every day for five years? I've been stuck in this hellhole, trying to find a way out, trying to survive. And you... you just arrived. You have no idea what it's like."

Lena shifted uncomfortably next to me, glancing between Sarah and me. I could see the confusion in her eyes, the uncertainty about what to think. I wasn't sure what to think either.

"So what?" I asked, my voice hard. "You decided to work with the Reptilians? You just... gave up?"

Sarah shook her head, her eyes flashing with frustration. "I didn't give up. I was trying to survive. I was *this close* to getting back to Earth. They promised me a way out. If I could help them with the Stargate, they said they'd let me return to Area 51."

I felt my anger rising, boiling under the surface. "And you believed them? You really thought the Reptilians would just *let* you go?"

She didn't answer, but the look in her eyes told me everything I needed to know. She had been desperate, clinging to any hope, no matter how slim or dangerous. And in that desperation, she had made choices—choices that had led to her standing alongside the very creatures that had tormented us.

"I know it sounds stupid," she said quietly, her voice trembling. "But I didn't see any other way. I've been trapped here for years, Ethan. Every day, I watched people die, watched them suffer. I just... I just wanted to go home."

Her words hit me like a punch to the gut. I'd only been in this hell for a few days, but Sarah had been here for five years. Five years of isolation, fear, and desperation. I couldn't imagine what that had done to her, what kind of mental and emotional scars she carried.

"But that's not all, is it?" Lena asked suddenly, her voice soft but steady. "You didn't just want to go back. You wanted to help the green race too, didn't you?"

Sarah's eyes flicked toward Lena, surprise flashing across her face. For a moment, she didn't say anything, but then she let out a long breath and nodded.

"Yes," she admitted, her voice barely above a whisper. "That's part of it too."

She leaned forward, resting her elbows on her knees, her hands clasped tightly together. "The Reptilians control everything here. The green race—they're slaves, trapped in these villages, working for the Reptilians, barely surviving. I thought... I thought if I could help the Reptilians, maybe I could find a way to help the green race too. I thought... maybe I could turn the tables on them."

I furrowed my brow, trying to make sense of what she was saying. "So, you wanted to steal the Stargate and use it against them?"

Sarah nodded, her face etched with guilt"I figured if I could get my hands on the Stargate, I could use it to destabilize the Reptilians' control and return to Earth. I could've gone back—our Earth—because it only had one shot, and after that, it wouldn't work. But when I saw you two in that facility, when I saw what they were doing to you..."

Her voice cracked, and she looked down at her hands. "I couldn't just stand there and do nothing. I had to help you."

The weight of her words settled over us like a thick blanket, and for a moment, none of us spoke. I could see the turmoil in Sarah's eyes, the pain and regret that had been building up inside her for years. She had made terrible choices, but she had also been trapped, just like us.

Lena spoke first, her voice soft but steady. "Sarah... we understand. You were doing what you thought you had to do to survive."

Sarah's eyes flickered with surprise. "You... you're not angry?"

Lena shook her head. "I'm not saying I agree with everything you did, but I understand why you did it. And right now, we need each other. The Reptilians are after all of us."

Sarah let out a shaky breath, her shoulders slumping with relief. "Thank you."

I crossed my arms, still feeling the tension in my chest, but I knew Lena was right. We couldn't afford to hold grudges. Not here. Not now. We had bigger problems to deal with.

"We need to focus on the green race," I said finally, my voice firm. "We need to help them fight back against the Reptilians."

Sarah nodded, her expression serious. "There's a resistance. It's small, and they've been keeping to the shadows, but they're there. They've been planning an uprising for years, but they need help. They need people who know how to fight, who can think strategically."

Lena glanced at me, her eyes filled with determination. "We can help them. We've seen the Reptilians' technology up close. We know how they operate."

Sarah stood up, her face set with resolve. "Then we need to get out of this village. The Reptilians will come looking for us, and it's only a matter of time before they find us. There's a tunnel system that the resistance has been using—it runs beneath the villages and connects to the cities. If we can reach it, we can hide there and plan our next move."

Lena and I stood as well, the firelight casting long shadows across the ground.

"Then let's go," I said, my voice steady. "We've got a revolution to plan."

Into the Tunnel

The village had grown eerily quiet as we prepared to leave. The green-skinned villagers moved about with nervous energy, their eyes flicking toward the sky as though they expected the Reptilians to descend at any moment. I could feel the tension in the air—the fear that had taken root in these people after years of oppression.

Sarah led us through the narrow streets, her movements quick and purposeful. She seemed to know exactly where she was going, her eyes scanning the darkened alleys and shadowy corners for any signs of danger.

"Where's this tunnel?" Lena asked, her voice hushed as we walked.

"It's hidden beneath one of the old storage houses," Sarah explained, her eyes focused on the path ahead. "The Reptilians don't know about it—at least, not yet. The resistance has been using it to move supplies and people in and out of the villages for years."

I glanced around the village, my heart pounding in my chest. Every shadow seemed to hold the threat of discovery, every rustle of the wind sent a shiver down my spine. We couldn't afford to be caught. Not now.

Finally, we reached a small, dilapidated building at the edge of the village. It looked abandoned, the wooden planks of the walls rotting and splintered, the roof sagging in the middle. Sarah led us inside, pushing open the door with a creak. The interior was dark, the air thick with the smell of damp wood and dust.

"Here," she whispered, kneeling down and pulling aside a section of the floorboards.

Beneath the boards was a narrow, stone staircase leading down into the darkness. A faint breeze drifted up from the tunnel, cool and damp, carrying with it the scent of earth and stone.

Lena hesitated for a moment, her eyes wide as she stared into the dark tunnel. "How far does it go?"

"Far enough," Sarah replied, her voice low. "It connects to a network of tunnels that run beneath the Reptilian cities. We'll be safe there, at least for a while."

I nodded, stepping forward and descending the staircase. The walls of the tunnel were damp, the stone cold beneath my fingers as I reached out to steady myself. The air grew cooler the farther we went, the sound of our footsteps echoing softly in the narrow passage.

We moved in silence for what felt like hours, the weight of the situation pressing down on us. Every now and then, I would glance back at Sarah, wondering if she was leading us to safety—or into another trap.

But as we reached a wide, open cavern deep beneath the ground, I saw the flicker of torchlight ahead, and a sense of hope stirred in my chest.

The resistance was real. And we were about to meet them.

The Resistance

The flickering torchlight cast long, wavering shadows along the damp stone walls of the cavern. The cold, underground air filled my lungs as I stepped into the wide-open space beneath the earth, my eyes adjusting to the dim light. Lena and Sarah followed closely behind me, their footsteps echoing softly in the vast tunnel.

The cavern was much larger than I had expected. It stretched far beyond what I could see, the walls disappearing into the shadows. Rough-hewn pillars of stone supported the ceiling, and small clusters of green-skinned villagers huddled near the flickering torches, their faces drawn and pale.

These were the people of the resistance—the ones who had been hiding in the shadows for years, waiting for their moment to strike back against the Reptilians.

But as I looked around, I realized just how few of them there were. Maybe a couple dozen at most. Their eyes were hollow, their expressions weary, their clothes torn and ragged. These weren't soldiers—they were survivors. And they looked broken.

Sarah moved ahead of us, her movements quick and purposeful, as if she were familiar with the place. She nodded to a few of the villagers as she passed, and they nodded back, their faces showing a flicker of recognition. It was clear that she had been here before—that she had worked with these people, even while pretending to collaborate with the Reptilians.

Lena glanced around the cavern, her eyes wide with a mix of awe and uncertainty. "This is the resistance?"

Sarah stopped and turned to face us, her expression serious. "It's all that's left."

I could hear the weight in her voice, the exhaustion. She had been fighting this war for years, and the toll it had taken on her was clear.

But now, as we stood in the heart of the resistance's hidden sanctuary, I realized just how dire the situation truly was.

"They've been fighting the Reptilians for years," Sarah explained, her voice low. "But the Reptilians have the upper hand. They have the technology, the weapons, the numbers. The green race... they've been holding on by a thread."

I frowned, my heart sinking as I looked at the weary faces of the villagers around us. They looked like they hadn't eaten in days, their bodies frail and emaciated from years of oppression. How could they possibly hope to fight against the Reptilians, let alone win?

Lena stepped forward, her brow furrowed in concern. "Is this all of them?"

Sarah shook her head. "No. There are more—scattered across the villages, hiding in the tunnels, waiting for their chance. But most of them are afraid. They've seen what happens when someone tries to resist. The Reptilians crush any sign of rebellion before it even begins."

I clenched my fists, anger bubbling beneath the surface. "Then we need to give them hope. We need to show them that they can fight back."

Sarah nodded, her eyes hardening with determination. "That's why we're here. The Stargate... it's our only chance."

"Sarah," the Stargate only works one way. How did you use it to get us back here?"

Sarah's pacing stopped, and for a moment, she didn't meet my eyes. The shadows under her eyes spoke of exhaustion and the burden of too many secrets. Finally, she let out a long breath, her shoulders sagging.

"The Stargate does work both ways," she admitted, her voice barely above a whisper. "The Controllers can use it to travel anywhere in the realm, and they've shared that technology with the Reptilians. That's why the Reptilians are so obsessed with it. They think it's a gateway to other realms, other places of power. But it's more than that—it's the key to controlling movement within our world."

I blinked, my mind racing. "You mean... they've been using it all along? Why didn't they tell me?"

Sarah's expression darkened. "Because you, Ethan, are a problem to them. They know you opened the Stargate in the first place. They're afraid you'll figure out how it works—afraid you'll be able to use it in ways they can't predict or control."

The realization hit me like a punch to the gut. That was why they'd captured us. Not just because they wanted information about NASA or the Stargate—but because they feared what I could do with it.

"They've been using the Stargate to move through the realm, controlling everything from behind the scenes," Sarah continued. "But the Reptilians still don't fully understand it. They think it's connected to some greater power, and that's where their obsession lies. If we can make them believe that you've figured out how to unlock its full potential, they'll panic. And that's when we strike."

I narrowed my eyes, skepticism creeping into my voice. "You really think that'll work? That they'll believe I've figured out something they haven't?"

"They've underestimated you before," Sarah said, her eyes gleaming with intensity. "They're arrogant. They think they have everything under control, but you're an anomaly. You opened the Stargate once, and they know you could do it again—only this time, on your terms."

I glanced at Lena, who was standing silently beside me, her expression thoughtful. She caught my eye and nodded slowly. "It's risky," she said softly, "but it might be the only chance we have."

Sarah stepped closer, her voice lowering to a whisper. "But there's more. The Reptilians aren't just watching us from the outside. They've been watching us from within. They have spies—shape-shifters—who've been blending in with the villages for years. We can't trust anyone until we're sure. We can't let them know what we're planning."

A cold chill ran down my spine. Shape-shifters. It made sense. We'd already seen the Reptilians' ability to manipulate reality, to twist memories and emotions. If they could infiltrate the resistance without us knowing... we wouldn't stand a chance.

"So how do we know who we can trust?" I asked, my voice tight with anxiety.

Sarah sighed, running a hand through her hair. "We don't. That's the problem. But we need to be cautious. Careful about who we tell, how we move forward. The Reptilians are waiting for us to make a mistake, and they'll use it to crush us if we're not careful."

I clenched my fists, the weight of the situation pressing down on me. The stakes had never been higher, and there was so much at risk—so many lives hanging in the balance. One wrong move, and everything would be lost.

"We'll need to use their obsession with the Stargate against them," I said finally, my voice steady. "But we have to be smart. If we're going to win this, we need to stay two steps ahead of them."

Sarah nodded, her face grim. "Agreed. But we can't wait long. The Reptilians will come looking for us, and they'll bring their full force when they do."

I turned to Lena, who was watching the conversation with quiet intensity. "You're right," she said. "This is our only shot."

Preparing for the Uprising

Over the next few days, the tunnels beneath the village became a hive of activity. The green-skinned villagers, the last remnants of the resistance, began gathering supplies, sharpening weapons, and preparing for the coming battle. Word had spread quickly, and more villagers were slipping through the cracks, finding their way to the hidden tunnels beneath the city. The resistance was small and scattered, but it was growing.

As the preparations ramped up, I found myself in a role I had never expected to take on—leader. It was strange. I'd always been a scientist, focused on research and discovery, not someone who led uprisings or fought wars. But now, as the resistance looked to me for guidance, I realized there was no turning back. They saw me as a symbol, a beacon of hope, someone who could help them turn the tide against the Reptilians.

The responsibility weighed heavily on my shoulders, but I couldn't let them down.

Lena was by my side every step of the way. She threw herself into the preparations, helping the villagers fortify their positions, building makeshift weapons, and coordinating supply runs. Her resourcefulness and quick thinking were keeping the resistance alive, and I couldn't have done any of this without her.

Sarah, meanwhile, worked tirelessly with the resistance's few remaining leaders, helping them strategize and plan the attack. Her knowledge of the Reptilians' operations—gained during her years of working within their system—was invaluable. Despite the tension between us, I knew we needed her. Without her insights, we wouldn't stand a chance.

The cavern beneath the village became a makeshift headquarters for the uprising. Villagers moved in and out of the tunnels, carrying weapons, supplies, and messages from the other scattered groups that had yet to join the fight. The air was thick with anticipation—and fear. Everyone knew what was at stake. Everyone knew that if we failed, the Reptilians would wipe us out completely. There would be no second chances.

One evening, as the sun set beyond the horizon and the cavern was illuminated by the warm glow of torches, I stood with Lena and Sarah near the entrance to the tunnels. The cool air filled my lungs, and the soft murmur of the villagers working echoed through the space.

Lena broke the silence, her brow furrowed with concern. "Do you really think we can do this?"

I hesitated, unsure of how to answer. I wanted to tell her we would win, that we would defeat the Reptilians and free the green race from their oppression. But I couldn't. The Reptilians were powerful—far more powerful than anything we had ever faced. Our chances of victory were slim, and we all knew it.

But we didn't have a choice.

"We have to try," I said finally, my voice steady. "We can't let them win."

Lena nodded, her eyes filled with determination. "You're right. We have to."

Sarah stepped forward, her face set with grim resolve. The Reptilians aren't invincible. They've made mistakes before. They underestimated the green race, and they've underestimated us. That's their weakness. And now we know—they've been controlling our region, Earth, from behind the scenes all along.

I glanced at her, surprised by the conviction in her voice. "And you think we can exploit that?"

Sarah nodded. "Yes. We can. But we need to be smart. We need to strike at the right moment, when they're vulnerable. The Controllers may be using the Stargate to keep control of the realm, but they've put too much faith in the Reptilians. That's our advantage."

Lena folded her arms, her gaze distant. "And when will that be?"

Sarah hesitated, her eyes flicking to the ground. "Soon. Very soon. We need to be ready."

I felt a knot of anxiety tighten in my chest. The uprising was coming—whether we were ready or not—and the fate of the resistance, of the entire green race, rested on our shoulders.

But as I looked around at the villagers, at their tired but determined faces, I knew one thing for sure.

We weren't alone. And together, we stood a chance.

The Science of War

The cavern was quiet except for the soft hum of energy pulsing through the air—a mix of the preparations for the impending battle and the tension that was thick enough to cut with a knife. I sat in the small, makeshift lab the resistance had set up for me in a corner of the underground base, staring at the dissection table in front of me. The body of a Reptilian lay before me, cold and still, its scales catching the faint glow of the torches lining the walls.

The others were in the tunnels, gathering supplies and fortifying our defenses, but I couldn't stop thinking about the Reptilians, about how they worked, how they fought. Something about them had always felt off—something I hadn't been able to put my finger on until now.

I'd never been a soldier. I was a scientist, trained to solve problems through logic and analysis, not to lead armies or fight wars. But now, I had no choice. If we were going to survive, if we were going to have any hope of defeating the Reptilians, I needed to find a way to fight them on their own terms.

The Reptilian corpse in front of me was one of the few we had managed to kill during our escape. Their bodies were tough, their reflexes sharp, and their ability to shape-shift had given them the upper hand in nearly every encounter. But I had a feeling that their power—this ability to change form—was also their greatest weakness. I just had to figure out how.

Lena entered the lab quietly, carrying a tray of equipment we'd scavenged from one of the underground stores. Her eyes met mine, and she gave me a soft smile, though I could see the weariness etched across her face. We were all running on borrowed time, and every minute that passed brought us closer to the inevitable clash with the Reptilians.

"You've been at this for hours," she said, setting the tray down beside me. "Any luck?"

I sighed, rubbing a hand across my forehead. "Not yet. But there's something here. I can feel it. They're not invincible, Lena. There's a pattern to how they change, to how they manipulate their appearance. If I can figure out how their shape-shifting works, we might be able to exploit it."

Lena nodded, pulling up a stool to sit beside me. "If anyone can figure it out, it's you."

Her faith in me was reassuring, but I couldn't shake the pressure that weighed down on my shoulders. The resistance was counting on me, and failure wasn't an option. We had to find a way to reveal the Reptilian spies among us before they tore us apart from the inside.

I leaned over the body on the table, studying the intricate patterns of its scaly skin. The Reptilian's body was humanoid, but there were clear differences—subtle variations in muscle structure, the density of their skin, and most importantly, the strange nodes I had found embedded beneath the surface of its throat. These nodes were the key. I was sure of it.

I carefully inserted the tip of my scalpel into one of the nodes, peeling back the skin to reveal a cluster of delicate tissue and what looked like a small, metallic implant nestled within. I frowned, leaning closer.

"What is that?" Lena asked, her voice hushed.

"I'm not sure," I replied, squinting as I inspected the implant. "It looks like some kind of bio-technology. It's fused with the organic tissue, but it doesn't belong here naturally. My guess is this implant is what allows them to shift their forms."

Lena's brow furrowed. "You think they're using technology to shape-shift?"

"Partially, yes," I said, carefully removing the implant with a pair of tweezers. "Their shape-shifting ability isn't purely biological. They use some kind of frequency to alter their appearance, and this implant is how they control it."

I held up the small, metallic device, turning it over in my hand. It was no bigger than a coin, but I could feel the faint hum of energy pulsing from within.

"If we can figure out the frequency they use," I continued, my mind racing, "we might be able to disrupt it. We could reveal them for what they are—force them to drop their disguises."

Lena's eyes widened. "That would change everything. If we could expose the shape-shifters hiding among us…"

"They wouldn't be able to hide anymore," I finished, a surge of excitement building in my chest. "We could level the playing field."

Lena nodded, her expression serious. "But how do we find the right frequency? We can't just guess."

I set the implant down and reached for a small, handheld scanner—another piece of equipment we'd scavenged from the tunnels. I powered it on and ran it over the implant, watching as the screen lit up with a series of readings.

"We don't have to guess," I said, my eyes fixed on the data. "If we can isolate the frequency from this implant, we can build a device to disrupt it. It's just a matter of time."

Lena watched me work in silence for a few moments, then spoke softly. "You've really thought this through, haven't you?"

I glanced at her, a small smile tugging at the corner of my lips. "I've had a lot of time to think. This is our best chance."

She returned the smile, though there was a hint of sadness in her eyes. "I just hope it's enough."

We fell into a comfortable silence as I continued to scan the implant, the data slowly coming together on the screen. The more I analyzed it, the more certain I became. The Reptilians' shape-shifting ability was controlled by a specific frequency, one that could be disrupted if we had the right technology.

After a few more minutes, the scanner beeped, and the screen displayed the final result.

"There," I said, pointing to the frequency on the screen. "That's it. That's what they use to change their forms."

Lena leaned in, her eyes scanning the data. "So, now what?"

"Now," I said, my mind racing, "we build something to disrupt it. If we can create a device that emits this frequency, we can force them to reveal themselves. It won't hurt them, but it'll break their disguise."

Lena's eyes widened, her excitement growing. "That would change everything. If we can expose the shape-shifters hiding in the resistance, we can stop them from sabotaging us."

I nodded, my heart pounding with the weight of the realization. This was it. This was the key to turning the tide of the battle. If we could reveal the Reptilians hiding among us, we could eliminate the threat from within and focus on the larger fight ahead.

But as the excitement coursed through me, a darker thought crept into my mind. If the Reptilians had shape-shifters embedded in the resistance, how many of them were there? How long had they been hiding in plain sight, feeding information to their masters?

Lena seemed to sense my unease. "What's wrong?"

I looked up at her, my voice low. "We need to be prepared. There could be more shape-shifters among us than we realize. If we expose them, we'll be putting a target on our backs."

She nodded, her expression serious. "But we have no choice, right?"

"Right," I agreed. "This is our only shot."

Unmasking the Enemy

Two days later, we stood in the heart of the resistance's main hideout, a large underground chamber lined with weapons, supplies, and makeshift beds. The air was thick with tension as the members of the resistance gathered around, their green skin illuminated by the glow of the torches that lined the walls.

Sarah stood next to me, her arms crossed, her face set with grim determination. Lena was beside her, her eyes scanning the crowd as we prepared for what was about to happen. I could feel the weight of the device in my hand—the small emitter we had built to disrupt the Reptilians' shape-shifting frequency.

"If this works," I said quietly, "we'll know exactly who we can trust."

Sarah nodded. "And if it doesn't?"

I swallowed hard, my throat dry. "Then we're dead."

Lena took a deep breath, her voice steady but laced with nerves. "Let's do it."

I stepped forward, the emitter in my hand, and raised my voice to address the crowd. "We've all been through hell. We've lost friends, family, and nearly everything we've ever known. But we're not done fighting. Not yet."

The crowd murmured in agreement, their eyes filled with a mix of hope and fear.

"But there's something we need to deal with first," I continued. "There are Reptilian spies among us—shape-shifters who have been hiding in plain sight, feeding information back to the enemy."

Gasps rippled through the crowd, fear and suspicion flashing across their faces.

I held up the emitter. "This device will reveal them. It won't hurt anyone, but it'll force the shape-shifters to show their true form."

The crowd was silent, their eyes fixed on the small device in my hand.

"We need to do this," I said, my voice firm. "If we're going to survive, if we're going to win this fight, we need to know who's really on our side."

For a moment, no one spoke. The air was thick with tension, and I could feel the weight of every gaze on me. Then, slowly, one of the resistance members stepped forward—a young woman with wide, fearful eyes.

"Do it," she said, her voice trembling but resolute. "If there are spies among us, we need to know."

One by one, the others nodded in agreement, their faces pale but determined.

I took a deep breath, my heart pounding in my chest, and activated the emitter.

A low hum filled the air, and a wave of energy swept through the chamber. For a moment, nothing happened. The members of the resistance stood frozen, their eyes wide with fear.

Then, suddenly, four figures began to shimmer, their forms flickering like static on a broken television. The crowd gasped as the illusion shattered, revealing the true forms of the Reptilian shape-shifters among us. Their green, scaly skin gleamed in the torchlight, their yellow eyes wide with shock and fury.

For a heartbeat, no one moved. Then chaos erupted.

The resistance members closest to the Reptilians lunged at them, weapons raised, while the shape-shifters fought back with brutal strength. The chamber descended into a frenzy of violence, the air thick with the sound of metal clashing and the cries of battle.

Lena grabbed my arm, her voice urgent. "We need to get out of here!"

I nodded, my heart racing. The battle had begun, and there was no turning back now.

As we fought our way through the chaos, I couldn't shake the feeling that everything had changed—that the battle for survival had just taken a dark, irreversible turn. We had unmasked the enemy, but in doing so, we had unleashed something far more dangerous.

The war was no longer just about survival. It was about annihilation.

Breaking the Enemy

The captured Reptilians lay on the cold stone floor of the cavern, bound and gagged, their scaly forms glinting in the flickering torchlight. The resistance had never captured a Reptilian alive before, and the air in the room crackled with the tense energy of this unprecedented moment. For so long, they had fought these shape-shifting creatures, suffering loss after loss. But now—now, we had them.

I stood at the edge of the room, watching as the resistance members carefully checked the restraints on the Reptilians. Their yellow eyes darted around, filled with a mixture of rage and fear. They writhed against the ropes, hissing and snarling, but they weren't going anywhere.

Sarah stood beside me, her expression hard as stone, while Lena busied herself with adjusting the small frequency emitter that we'd used to reveal the shape-shifters earlier. The discovery had been a game changer—this frequency could force them to show their true form, but with a higher intensity, it could do more.

I approached the restrained Reptilians, my mind racing with the possibilities. We were on the verge of something big—something that could shift the balance of power in this war.

"Are we sure this will work?" Lena asked, glancing up at me from where she knelt beside the emitter. Her voice was calm, but I could see the tension in her eyes.

I nodded slowly. "We know that this frequency affects their ability to maintain their shape-shifting. But it's more than that. The implant I found in their bodies—it's not just for altering appearance. It's connected to their nervous system, controlling how they interact with the world around them. With the right intensity, we might be able to… influence them."

Sarah's brow furrowed as she studied the captured Reptilians. "You mean... mind control?"

I met her gaze and nodded. "That's exactly what I mean. They've been using it against us for years. It's time we turned the tables."

The room was silent for a moment, the weight of my words settling over the gathered resistance fighters. Some of them looked uncertain, others eager to see their enemy suffer for once.

"We need answers," I continued, turning back to the Reptilians. "We need to know how the Stargate works—how they control it, how they move between realms. And if this frequency can help us get that information, then we have to use it."

Lena stood up, the emitter now ready in her hands. "Let's find out."

I motioned for the others to step back as I crouched beside one of the restrained Reptilians. The creature glared up at me, its reptilian pupils narrowing to slits, but it couldn't mask the fear in its eyes.

"Hold still," I said, my voice cold. "This is going to hurt."

I gave Lena a nod, and she activated the emitter.

A low, vibrating hum filled the room, and the Reptilian beneath me convulsed, its body jerking violently as the frequency intensified. It let out a choked, guttural cry, its muscles twitching as the sound waves resonated through its body.

The other Reptilians began to writhe as well, their bodies reacting to the frequency, but we held firm. We weren't going to let up until we had the information we needed.

"Turn it up," I ordered.

Lena adjusted the emitter, and the intensity of the frequency increased. The Reptilian beneath me screamed, its voice high-pitched and distorted, as though it were being torn apart from the inside. Its yellow eyes rolled back in its head, and for a moment, I thought it might die from the pain. But then, slowly, it stopped resisting.

I leaned closer, my voice low and steady. "You know what we want. Tell us how the Stargate works—both ways."

For a moment, it was silent. The Reptilian's chest heaved as it gasped for breath, but then, slowly, it began to speak. Its voice was hoarse, broken by the pain, but it was clear enough for us to understand.

"The Stargate... is controlled... by the Controllers..." it hissed, its body trembling. "The Reptilians... we use it... to travel... between the areas... but only... with permission."

I exchanged a glance with Lena. This was exactly what we needed to know.

"How?" I pressed, my voice sharp. "How do you use it? How can we control it?"

The Reptilian's eyes flicked toward me, filled with hatred, but it was too weak to resist any longer. "The Stargate... is linked... to the frequencies... that control us. The Controllers... they have the master key... but you... you have the device... the emitter. With it... you could... disrupt the control... override the system..."

I felt my heart race as the realization hit me. The emitter we had built to expose their shape-shifting—it could do more than that. It could disrupt their entire control system.

"You're saying we can control the Stargate ourselves?" I asked, my voice filled with disbelief.

The Reptilian nodded weakly. "Yes... but only if... you find the right frequency... you could... take control... of the gate."

I stood up, my mind racing. This was it. This was the breakthrough we needed. We could control the Stargate. We could move between areas. And with that power, we could finally stand a chance against the Reptilians and the Controllers.

"Turn it off," I said quietly to Lena. She deactivated the emitter, and the room was suddenly filled with silence once more.

The captured Reptilians lay motionless, their bodies still trembling from the effects of the frequency. But it didn't matter. We had what we needed.

The First Battle

The resistance had never launched a direct attack on the Reptilian cities before. They had always stayed in the shadows, striking from hidden locations, using guerrilla tactics to avoid being crushed by the overwhelming power of their enemies. But now, everything had changed.

We stood in the narrow tunnels beneath the Reptilian city, the air thick with tension as the resistance fighters prepared for their first true battle. The frequency weapons we had built—small, portable emitters that could disrupt the Reptilians' shape-shifting abilities—were strapped to the belts of every fighter. This was our trump card. This was how we would win.

Sarah stood beside me, her face set with determination. Lena was on my other side, her eyes scanning the darkness ahead, ready for the fight that was about to begin.

"We've never done anything like this before," Lena whispered, her voice tight with anxiety.

I nodded, my heart pounding in my chest. "I know. But we're ready. We have the weapons, and we have the element of surprise."

Sarah glanced at me, her voice steady. "The Reptilians aren't expecting us to attack their city. They think we're too weak, too disorganized. But they don't know what we've learned."

I tightened my grip on my own frequency emitter. "We'll show them."

We moved forward, the sound of our footsteps muffled by the soft earth beneath us. The tunnel led directly into the heart of the Reptilian city, a sprawling, high-tech metropolis that had stood untouched for centuries. The Reptilians had ruled this land with an iron fist, crushing any resistance that dared to rise against them.

But now, for the first time, we were fighting back.

As we reached the edge of the tunnel, I signaled for the others to stop. The entrance to the city was just ahead, a wide metal door that led into the sprawling underground complex where the Reptilians lived and worked.

I took a deep breath, steeling myself for what was about to happen.

"Ready?" I whispered.

Lena nodded. "Ready."

Sarah gave me a determined look. "Let's do this."

I activated the frequency emitter, and the low hum filled the air. The sound reverberated through the walls of the tunnel, and I could feel the power of it vibrating in my bones.

"Go," I ordered.

The metal door slid open, and we rushed into the city.

The Reptilians were caught completely off guard. They hadn't expected us to bring the fight to their doorstep, and as we poured into the city, the resistance fighters unleashed their frequency weapons. The Reptilians' shape-shifting abilities were immediately disrupted, their bodies flickering and convulsing as the emitters broke through their defenses.

For the first time, the resistance wasn't running. We were fighting, and we were winning.

Lena moved beside me, her frequency emitter blazing as she fought off a group of Reptilian soldiers. Sarah was on the other side of the street, leading another group of fighters as they pushed deeper into the city.

The battle was chaotic, the air filled with the sounds of gunfire, screams, and the hum of the frequency weapons. But for the first time, the green-skinned villagers—the resistance—were holding their ground.

I watched as the Reptilians fell back, their forces crumbling under the onslaught of the frequency weapons. For so long, they had relied on their ability to shift forms, to manipulate and control, but now that power had been taken from them. They were vulnerable, exposed.

And we were taking full advantage of it.

The battle raged on for what felt like hours, the resistance pushing deeper into the city, overwhelming the Reptilian forces with every step. For the first time, I saw hope in the eyes of the fighters around me—hope that we could win, that we could take back what had been stolen from us.

Finally, as the sun began to set beyond the horizon, the last of the Reptilian soldiers fell. The city was ours.

The resistance had won its first battle.

The Turning Point

The battle had been won, but the war was far from over.

We stood in the heart of the Reptilian city, its towering buildings casting long shadows across the streets. The green-skinned villagers—once downtrodden and fearful—were now surging forward, their eyes blazing with newfound hope. For the first time in centuries, they had taken something back from their oppressors. They had won a battle, and the victory had ignited a fire in their hearts that would not be easily extinguished.

The Reptilian forces had fallen back, retreating into the shadows, leaving their once-impenetrable city vulnerable. The air was thick with the scent of burning metal and scorched earth, and the distant sound of small skirmishes echoed through the streets. But for the most part, the city was ours.

Lena stood beside me, her chest heaving with exhaustion but her eyes alight with victory. She wiped the sweat from her brow, a triumphant smile tugging at the corners of her lips.

"We did it," she breathed, her voice filled with disbelief.

I nodded, still trying to wrap my mind around the fact that we had won. The frequency weapons had worked. The Reptilians' shape-shifting abilities had been stripped away, leaving them vulnerable for the first time in centuries. And we had taken full advantage of it.

But even as the resistance celebrated their victory, I couldn't shake the nagging thought at the back of my mind. This was just the beginning. The Reptilians were powerful, and their defeat here, while significant, was only a small step in a much larger war. We had won the battle, but the war against the Controllers—the true rulers of this realm—was far from over.

I glanced at Sarah, who was standing a few feet away, talking quietly with a group of resistance leaders. Her face was grim, her expression hard. She had been instrumental in helping us win this battle, but I could see the weight of everything we had learned bearing down on her.

The Stargate. The key to everything.

For so long, the Reptilians had guarded the secrets of the Stargate, using it to move between realms, controlling the flow of power across the boundaries of our world. But now, we had the knowledge—and the technology—to use it for ourselves. The frequency emitters we had built, the small devices we had used to expose the Reptilians' shape-shifting abilities, were more powerful than we had realized. With the right adjustments, we could control the Stargate. We could move between realms, just as the Reptilians and the Controllers had done for centuries.

But the question remained: What would we do with that power?

As if sensing my thoughts, Lena stepped closer, her voice low. "You're thinking about the Stargate, aren't you?"

I nodded, my gaze drifting toward the distant horizon. "Yeah. We have the knowledge now. We could use it."

"And go back to Earth," she said softly.

The weight of her words settled over me like a heavy blanket. Earth. Home. For so long, we had been trapped in this alien realm, fighting for survival, trying to understand the rules of this strange, fragmented world. But now, we had the means to return. To go back to Area 51, back to our own people.

But it wasn't that simple. Nothing ever was.

"I can rebuild the device," I said quietly, my mind already racing with the possibilities. "I know how it works now. We can use the frequency to control the Stargate, open it from both sides."

Lena's eyes widened, a spark of hope flickering in their depths. "You can really do it?"

"I can," I replied. "It'll take time, a few days at least, but I can build the device."

Her face softened, a mixture of relief and apprehension crossing her features. "We could go home."

I nodded, the thought filling me with a strange mix of excitement and dread. "Yeah. We could."

But even as the words left my mouth, I felt the weight of the decision settling over me. Going home meant leaving behind everything we had fought for here. It meant abandoning the resistance, abandoning the green-skinned villagers who had risked everything to fight back against the Reptilians.

I glanced over at Sarah, who was still deep in conversation with the resistance leaders. She had been here for years, fighting, surviving, waiting for a chance to make a difference. And now, she had found it.

I wasn't sure if I could leave her behind.

Building the Device

The next few days passed in a blur of activity. While the resistance continued to secure their hold on the city, I locked myself away in a small workshop, surrounded by parts and tools scavenged from the Reptilian technology. The frequency emitter sat in front of me on the workbench, its sleek, metallic surface gleaming under the harsh light of the overhead lamps.

I had dismantled the original emitter we had used to disrupt the Reptilians' shape-shifting abilities, studying every component, every wire, every circuit. It was a marvel of technology, a blend of organic and mechanical systems that worked in perfect harmony. And now, with the knowledge we had gained from the captured Reptilian, I was ready to take it a step further.

The Stargate was powered by frequencies—specific sound waves that interacted with the fabric of space and time, allowing the Reptilians and Controllers to move between realms. The device I was building would allow us to control those frequencies, to override the system and open the Stargate from both sides.

It was delicate work, and every moment was filled with the tension of knowing that a single mistake could mean failure. But failure wasn't an option. Not this time.

Lena was a constant presence at my side, helping me when she could, but mostly offering quiet support. She knew how important this was, not just for us, but for the future of the resistance. The device wasn't just a way for us to return home—it was a weapon. A tool that could turn the tide of the war.

On the third day, as I was adjusting the final settings on the emitter, Sarah entered the workshop. She looked tired, her eyes heavy with exhaustion, but there was a steely determination in her gaze.

"Is it ready?" she asked, her voice steady.

I nodded, holding up the device. "It's ready."

She exhaled softly, her eyes flicking to the emitter in my hands. "So, we're really going back."

I nodded, though there was an uncertainty in my heart. "That's the plan. We've done what we can here. It's time to return to Earth, to Area 51, and find a way to bring reinforcements."

Sarah's lips pressed into a thin line, and she looked away, her eyes clouded with something I couldn't quite place. "And you really think that's the best idea?"

I frowned, confusion flickering across my face. "Of course it is. We can get help from Earth. We have the technology now. With this, the resistance will be able to fight back."

Sarah was silent for a long moment, and then she looked up at me, her eyes filled with something I hadn't expected to see.

"I'm not going with you," she said quietly.

The words hit me like a punch to the gut. For a moment, I just stared at her, trying to process what she had said. "What?"

"I'm staying," she said, her voice stronger now, more certain. "I've been fighting this war for years, Ethan. I can't leave now. Not when we're finally starting to make progress."

I blinked, my mind racing. This wasn't what I had expected. I had thought that Sarah, after everything she had been through, would want to come back to Earth with us. That she would want to escape this place, leave the war behind.

But as I looked at her, standing there with that hard, determined look in her eyes, I realized I had been wrong.

"You're staying?" I repeated, my voice tinged with disbelief. "But... Sarah, we're going back to Earth. We can get help. We can end this."

She shook her head slowly. "I know. And that's why I need to stay. The green race—they need me. We've fought too hard, come too far, to abandon them now. I've spent years fighting for these people, trying to give them a chance at freedom. I can't leave them."

I felt my heart sink as the weight of her words settled over me. I had thought that the battle we had just won would be the end of it, that we would return to Earth and find a way to put this all behind us. But for Sarah, this wasn't the end. It was only the beginning.

Lena, who had been standing silently beside me, stepped forward, her voice soft. "You're sure about this, Sarah?"

Sarah nodded, her expression resolute. "I'm sure. This is where I belong now. This is my fight."

For a moment, none of us spoke. The air in the workshop was thick with the tension of everything that had been left unsaid.

Finally, I stepped forward, holding out the device I had built. "Then take this. You'll need it."

She looked down at the device in my hand, her eyes flicking between me and it. "What is it?"

"It's the same device we're using to control the Stargate," I explained. "With this, you'll be able to open it from either side. If things get too dangerous, if you ever need to leave... you'll have a way out."

Sarah's eyes softened, and for a moment, I saw a flicker of gratitude cross her face. She reached out, taking the device from my hand, her fingers brushing mine. "Thank you."

I nodded, my throat tight with emotion. "You've earned it. You've done more than anyone could have asked."

She gave me a small, sad smile. "So have you."

The Stargate

The moment had finally come. After days of preparation, after months of fighting for survival, we were standing before the Stargate once again. The massive structure loomed over us, its surface shimmering like liquid metal, rippling with energy as the frequency emitters hummed to life.

Lena stood beside me, her face pale but determined. We had made our choice. We were going back to Earth—back to Area 51—back to the life we had left behind.

But as I activated the device, as the Stargate flared to life and the swirling portal opened before us, I couldn't shake the feeling that this wasn't the end. We had won a battle here, but the war was far from over.

The Controllers were still out there, watching, waiting. And the Reptilians would regroup. They always did.

"We're really doing this," Lena whispered, her voice trembling with a mixture of excitement and fear.

I nodded, my heart pounding in my chest. "Yeah. We're doing it."

I turned to Sarah one last time. She stood at the edge of the platform, watching us with a quiet intensity. She gave me a small nod, and I returned it.

"Good luck," she called out over the hum of the Stargate.

"You too," I replied.

And with that, Lena and I stepped through the portal, the world around us dissolving into a swirl of light and sound.

We were going home.

The Return and the Chase

The swirling energy of the Stargate enveloped us, pulling Lena and me through the shimmering portal. The disorienting sensation of being stretched, twisted, and hurtled through space washed over us, making my heart race. But amidst the chaos, one thought kept me grounded—**we were finally going home.**

Home.

After everything we had been through—fighting the Reptilians, helping the green race, unlocking the secrets of the Stargate—finally, we were going back. Earth. Area 51. We had made it.

The blinding light and swirling energy surrounding us faded as quickly as it had appeared. We stumbled forward, the cold, familiar air of the Nevada desert filling my lungs as I hit solid ground. My knees buckled slightly from the transition, but I quickly regained my balance.

The arid landscape of Area 51 stretched out before us, with its endless plains of rocky terrain and dry scrub. It was the same secretive base we had left behind—hidden behind military security and a veil of conspiracy. But now, after everything we'd seen, Area 51 felt small, insignificant. The desert wind blew, carrying with it the scent of dry earth and a sense of eerie stillness.

Lena steadied herself beside me, breathing heavily as she gazed at the familiar surroundings. Her face was pale, a mixture of exhaustion and disbelief.

"We're back," she whispered. "We actually made it."

I nodded, feeling the weight of our journey settle over me. We had escaped Area 52, helped the resistance, and now returned with knowledge—and power—that could change everything. The frequency weapons strapped to our belts were proof of that. More than just devices, they were our only hope of revealing the truth.

But something was wrong. Even as the familiar landscape stretched out before us, I felt a knot of tension growing in my chest. A nagging feeling that something wasn't quite right.

Lena's hand gripped my arm. "Ethan... do you hear that?"

The hairs on the back of my neck stood up. My senses sharpened as I listened, and then I heard it—faint, but growing louder. Footsteps. Swift, heavy, and unnatural.

I turned sharply, and my heart dropped.

Emerging from the horizon, silhouetted against the harsh desert sun, were dark figures—Reptilians. Sleek, armored, and fast, their cold, calculating eyes locked onto us. They were coming for us, and they weren't alone. There were several of them, moving with deadly precision, like predators closing in on prey.

"They know," I muttered under my breath, horror settling in.

Lena's eyes widened in panic. "How? How could they know we're back already?"

I didn't need to answer her. The truth was obvious—the Controllers had been watching us, tracking us from the moment we set foot in Area 52. They knew everything. And now, they had sent their enforcers to eliminate us before we could expose the truth. We were a threat they couldn't afford to let live.

"We need to run!" I shouted, grabbing Lena's hand and pulling her with me as we turned and sprinted across the rocky desert.

The Reptilians were fast—too fast. Their footsteps pounded behind us, kicking up dust as they pursued us with relentless speed. My heart raced as the weight of our situation pressed down on me. The frequency weapons on our belts were our only advantage, but they wouldn't stop the Reptilians for long. We needed a way out—fast. "We fired at them with the frequency weapons, but it wasn't enough. There were too many of them. It was only a matter of time before we got caught."

"They're gaining on us!" Lena shouted, glancing back in terror. "Ethan, what do we do?"

I looked around frantically, but the barren desert offered no cover. There was nowhere to hide, nowhere to run. The Reptilians were closing in, their cold, reptilian eyes glowing with cruel intent. The knot of fear in my chest tightened. We couldn't outrun them forever.

And we couldn't go back to Area 52. The resistance wouldn't stand a chance if we led the Reptilians and Controllers there. The green race was barely surviving as it was. If the Reptilians found them, it would be a slaughter.

My hand instinctively went to the frequency device at my belt. An idea sparked in my mind—dangerous, desperate, but it was our only chance.

"Hold on!" I shouted, pulling the device free from my belt.

"What are you doing?" Lena asked, panic rising in her voice as we continued to run.

"I'm going to open another portal," I replied, my fingers trembling as I adjusted the settings on the device. "I don't know where it'll take us, but anywhere is better than here!"

I quickly recalibrated the frequency, pushing the device to its limits. The air around us shimmered, rippling with energy as I focused on opening a new portal. Behind us, the Reptilians were getting closer, their hissing growls filling the air, their claws outstretched.

"Come on, come on," I muttered under my breath, willing the portal to open.

And then, just as the Reptilians were about to reach us, the air split open.

A shimmering vortex of light and energy erupted before us, its surface rippling like liquid glass. Without hesitation, I grabbed Lena's hand and leaped into the portal, the furious hisses of the Reptilians fading as the world dissolved into a kaleidoscope of light and sound.

The Unknown World

We tumbled out of the portal and landed hard on the ground. I gasped as the wind was knocked out of me, the shock of impact rattling my bones. My vision blurred for a moment, and I struggled to regain my bearings.

The air here was different—dense, thick, with an odd metallic taste on my tongue. I blinked, forcing my eyes to focus, and when they did, I froze in stunned silence.

We were no longer in the desert. In fact, we were no longer anywhere remotely familiar.

The world around us was like nothing I had ever seen before. The sky was a deep, shimmering silver, with swirling clouds that moved unnaturally fast, as if time itself was distorted. The ground beneath us was a smooth, reflective surface—like glass, but with a strange iridescent sheen that shifted and glimmered as we moved. It stretched out infinitely in every direction, creating the unsettling illusion that we were standing on the surface of a massive, endless mirror.

In the distance, massive, towering structures loomed—dark, angular shapes that pierced the sky like jagged monoliths. They weren't buildings, at least not in any sense that I could recognize. They were more like abstract, geometric forms, floating above the ground, their surfaces pulsing with a faint, glowing energy.

Lena slowly got to her feet beside me, her eyes wide with disbelief. "What... what is this place?"

"I don't know," I whispered, my voice barely audible. "But it's definitely not Earth."

We stood in silence for a moment, taking in the surreal, otherworldly landscape. There was no sound, no wind, no life. Just the strange, shimmering surface beneath us and the distant, eerie hum of the floating structures. It was like we had stepped into a world beyond time and space—a place that defied logic and reason.

Suddenly, a shadow passed overhead, and I looked up, my breath catching in my throat.

A massive creature soared above us, its silhouette dark against the silvery sky. At first, I thought it was some kind of bird, but as it circled lower, the sheer size of it became apparent.

It wasn't a bird.

It was a dragon.

The creature's enormous wings beat the air with a force that made the ground beneath us tremble. Its scales shimmered like polished steel, and its long, serpentine body coiled through the sky with a terrifying grace. Its eyes—glowing with an intense, fiery light—locked onto us, and I saw the flicker of flames gathering in its open maw.

"Ethan..." Lena's voice trembled with fear. "That's not a bird, is it?"

"No," I whispered, dread rising in my chest. "It's a dragon."

The dragon let out a deafening roar, the sound reverberating through the strange, mirrored landscape. Its massive jaws opened wide, and a torrent of fire erupted from its mouth, scorching the air as it hurtled toward us.

"Run!" I shouted, grabbing Lena's hand and pulling her with me as we sprinted across the mirrored ground.

The dragon's fire roared behind us, scorching the surface, sending waves of heat crashing into us. My heart pounded as we dodged between the towering structures, searching for any form of shelter. But there was none. The landscape stretched out endlessly, with no cover, no safety. The dragon swooped low, its massive wings casting a shadow over us as it prepared to strike again.

I glanced back, and my breath caught in my throat. The dragon was gaining on us, its eyes burning with fiery rage, its claws outstretched.

There was no time. No time to think. No time to plan.

We were out of options.

As the dragon's roar echoed through the strange, silent world, I tightened my grip on Lena's hand, praying that we would find a way out of this nightmare before it was too late.

Author's Note:

Thank you for joining me on this journey *Beyond the Ice Wall*. This story was born from my curiosity about the hidden realms and the untold truths that may lie just beyond our reach. I wanted to explore a world where the boundaries we take for granted—between the known and the unknown, reality and myth—begin to crumble. What would happen if everything we thought we knew about our world turned out to be a carefully crafted illusion?

It has been an adventure to imagine Dr. Cole and Lena's path as they uncover the mind-bending mysteries that lie hidden beyond the ice wall. I hope this story pulled you into the heart of their quest and kept you questioning the nature of reality along the way. If it sparked your imagination or left you wondering about what's truly out there, I'd love to hear your thoughts.

Your reviews mean the world to me and help other readers discover this tale. Please consider sharing your feedback on Amazon or Goodreads.

More to Come:

The journey doesn't end here. The mysteries revealed in *Beyond the Ice Wall* are just the beginning, and there's much more to discover. Stay tuned for the next chapter, as Dr. Cole and Lena continue to navigate a world where nothing is as it seems. Who knows what doors their next steps will open—or what they'll find waiting on the other side.

Until then, keep asking questions. Sometimes, the truth is closer than we think.

With gratitude,
[Mohamed Elshenawy]